WHO'S THERE?

Voices . . . she could hear voices up ahead! She froze in her tracks and listened again. All she could hear was her own heart, pounding double-time. Then the lights went out.

Inching along in the dark, she dragged her fingertips along the wall. One step . . . another . . . two more. Suddenly her hand bumped into something. It jerked out of her reach as soon as she'd made contact. "Who's there?" she demanded. She could hear someone breathing in short raspy breaths. Then something cool and thin, like wire, wrapped around her throat. It tightened quickly, cutting into the flesh. Jennifer gasped and choked, struggling for air. Clawing at the brittle noose but unable to force her fingers between it and her flesh, Jennifer fell to her knees. The wire tightened one final notch . . .

Voices . . . there were voices again in the distance . . . so far away she could barely make them out. *The last sounds I'll ever hear,* she thought sadly.

Other Avon Flare Books by
Nicole Davidson

CRASH COURSE
DEMON'S BEACH
WINTERKILL

Avon Books are available at special quantity discounts for bulk purchases for sales promotions, premiums, fund raising or educational use. Special books, or book excerpts, can also be created to fit specific needs.

For details write or telephone the office of the Director of Special Markets, Avon Books, Dept. FP, 1350 Avenue of the Americas, New York, New York 10019, 1-800-238-0658.

NICOLE DAVIDSON

If you purchased this book without a cover, you should be aware that this book is stolen property. It was reported as "unsold and destroyed" to the publisher, and neither the author nor the publisher has received any payment for this "stripped book."

THE STALKER is an original publication of Avon Books. This work has never before appeared in book form. This work is a novel. Any similarity to actual persons or events is purely coincidental.

AVON BOOKS
A division of
The Hearst Corporation
1350 Avenue of the Americas
New York, New York 10019

Copyright © 1992 by Kathryn Jensen
Published by arrangement with the author
Library of Congress Catalog Card Number: 92-93078
ISBN: 0-380-76645-0

All rights reserved, which includes the right to reproduce this book or portions thereof in any form whatsoever except as provided by the U.S. Copyright Law. For information address Columbia Literary Associates, 7902 Nottingham Way, Ellicott City, Maryland 21043.

First Avon Flare Printing: October 1992

AVON FLARE TRADEMARK REG. U.S. PAT. OFF. AND IN OTHER COUNTRIES, MARCA REGISTRADA, HECHO EN U.S.A.

Printed in the U.S.A.

RA 10 9 8 7 6 5 4 3 2 1

*For Linda Hayes
Of Columbia Literary Associates, Inc.—
a Great Agent and
a Dear Friend*

Chapter 1

"I've been deserted," Jennifer Merrill muttered under her breath as she wiped down the stainless steel countertop at Caramelbun.

As crew chief at the sweet roll shop in the mall she was responsible for leaving the place spotless when she locked up for the night. Unfortunately, her crew hadn't made it through the shift.

Mat Crosby had come down with some sort of flu. By nine o'clock he was running a fever and had excused himself twice to throw up in the men's room. She told him to go home. Then Marissa Larson's boyfriend showed up early and Marissa blew a gasket when Jennifer told her she couldn't leave until after closing at ten o'clock.

"Jerry *always* lets me leave early," Marissa complained. Jerry was their store manager.

"But he always has at least one other person staying with him to help close," Jennifer pointed out. "There's too much for me to do alone."

Marissa stared at her pleadingly, tears in her eyes. "Oh, please, Jen . . . just this once." She glanced over one shoulder at her boyfriend, who had just checked his watch for the third time and was now glaring impatiently at the two girls. "I'll make up the time, I promise. Pl-e-e-e-ease."

"Oh, all right. Go."

But now Jennifer regretted her decision. It wasn't the

work, although scrubbing down the counters with bleach, mopping the floor, and totaling the day's receipts was no joyride. She didn't like closing alone because then she'd have to walk out to the parking lot alone in the dark, and the things that went on at this hour at the mall were enough to frighten anyone.

McCarter Mall in the middle of East McCarter, Texas, might seem like any other all-American shopping center. The clothing, toy, shoe, athletic gear, electronics, candy, accessories, camera, and video shops spaced out between two glitzy department stores carried the same names as they would have at any other mall. The difference here was that a woman had been murdered among all these beautiful stores—and, six months later, no one knew who'd done it.

Looking up, Jennifer caught the eye of one of the security guards. He was dressed in a khaki uniform, with a walkie-talkie and ring of keys slung from his heavy belt. She didn't know his name; he was new and younger than the others . . . not much older than her eighteen years.

He stopped in front of Caramelbun and leaned over the counter. "You all right?" he asked, as if sensing her nervousness.

"Yeah. Fine," she said, removing her bright red apron and hanging it on a peg beside the huge ovens.

"All alone tonight?"

"It's no big deal. I've done it before."

His blond hair was trimly cut, and his eyes were the color of a winter sky. He wasn't particularly tall, but he wasn't short either. Jennifer thought he looked athletic, but in a relaxed way—not thick-necked like a jock.

"You work a lot of hours," he observed.

Propping the broom in a corner, she shrugged. "I like working at the mall."

The guard looked along the walkway at the electronics store, then back at her. "Your dad owns Super-Charged, doesn't he?"

"Yes, he does," she admitted proudly. "He carries the newest equipment on the market. Everything from the latest Walkman to CD changers, high power speakers, giant screen TVs—"

"Whoa," the guard said, laughing, "enough already. I've drooled at the displays every night for two months. I'm crazy about all kinds of electronic gadgets. They're kind of a hobby." He seemed to hesitate before asking, "Are you finished closing?"

"Well . . . almost." Jennifer took one last look around. An industrial-size tin of brown sugar had been left out. She replaced it in the storage room and locked the door. Picking up the canvas cash bag, she lifted a hinged section of the counter and stepped out of the shop.

"Sure you're okay on your own?" he asked.

Jennifer smiled. "My father's been bringing me to the mall to help out in his store since I was ten years old."

He grinned at her. "A real pro, huh? You must know every inch of this place and everything that goes on."

"Pretty much," Jennifer admitted. She pulled the security grate across the front of the shop and locked it with a key from her McCarter High chain.

"Want me to walk you to your car?" he offered.

"No thanks." Smiling, Jennifer started off down the deserted corridor. "I'll be fine." Any other day she would have jumped at the chance to be escorted to her car by a cute security guard. But tonight she was exhausted, knew she looked like hell, and suspected she smelled pretty revolting after long, sweaty hours with her head in the ovens.

After dropping off the bag in the night deposit slot at the bank, though, she admitted that she wasn't as sure of herself as she'd sounded a couple minutes earlier. Not another employee was in sight. Slowly she started moving along the deserted walkway.

Just then a flash of motion up ahead caught Jennifer's eye. She stopped and squinted, waiting for whatever it was to show itself again, but the line of stores remained perfectly motionless and quiet.

Nevertheless, a chill descended her spine. Strange things were rumored to happen at the mall . . . some of them explainable, others not. Like that poor old lady who'd been strangled.

The old lady, an older man, and a young woman, all dressed in rags, often hid out in the mall near closing time. Everyone said they were harmless, just homeless folks who slept in some remote corner of the mall. One morning a security guard found the older woman's body near the fountain.

Deciding she'd take a shortcut, Jennifer stepped into the narrow service corridor that ran between Super-Charged and Maxie's, the department store where her best friend worked. The tunnel was dark but familiar to her, its cement walls marred by occasional graffiti and by gouges where crates being brought in from the loading dock had scraped.

Her footsteps echoed, making it sound as if someone were following her. She glanced behind. Nothing. She walked faster anyway.

The police never found the killer, she reminded herself, and shivered at the thought.

The *McCarter News* had reported that the dead woman's name was Eleanor Duvall, originally from New Orleans. One reporter suggested she'd been killed by her comrades in a squabble over food or the best sleeping area. Others with more vivid imaginations claimed her killer stalked the mall at night in search of a new victim.

A soft scraping sound from up ahead made Jennifer stop to listen. Whatever had made the sound ceased. Probably a rat. Her father had complained to Mall Management several times about the filthy creatures. Her father's store shared a loading dock with a couple of other businesses. She used to play in the "secret passage" that connected the stores through their rear doors.

Slowly, Jennifer inched forward, her brain still working on old Eleanor. There were other possible explanations for her murder.

Every night, a guy showed up at the mall and hung out for the last half hour before closing in front of the video game arcade, trying to get the kids who came there to talk to him. Everyone said he was a drug pusher. Suppose that poor woman had walked in on a deal and seen something she wasn't supposed to see?

Or what about the sleazy couple who bought caseloads of beer in the nearest wet county and sold it in the parking lot near the north entrance? East McCarter was dry, but a lot of kids liked to party and were willing to pay double for a couple six packs or a keg.

One thing for sure; Jennifer didn't want to hang around any longer than she had to. She began to wish she'd taken the young security guard up on his offer.

But there was no turning back now. She'd feel like a fool chasing him down. Besides, in another two minutes she'd be out of here, safe in her car and on her way home.

Voices. She could hear voices up ahead! Not rats after all.

She froze in her tracks and listened again. The muffled conversation stopped. Now, all she could hear was her own heart pounding double-time in her chest.

Then the lights died.

It's just a power failure, she reassured herself. *Besides, I can find my way around here blindfolded.* Having come this far, she refused to go back.

Inching forward in the dark, she dragged her fingertips along one wall to help keep her balance. One step . . . another . . . two more. Sweat trickled down her upper lip, and the sensitive nerves along her spine began to prickle. She knew she must be close to the loading dock. From there she could run around the outside of the building to her car.

Her hand bumped into a stack of boxes. Reflexively, she reached out to steady them before they could fall over. Instead of finding cardboard, she grasped something covered in rough fabric.

An arm! she guessed, letting out a soft gasp of surprise.

The limb jerked out of her reach as soon as she'd made contact, but she sensed that the person it belonged to hadn't gone far.

"Who's there?" she demanded, her voice cracking, sounding eerily high pitched.

The person didn't move, didn't breathe. Jennifer peered into the darkness but was only able to make out a vague shape, a thicker patch of darkness against black space. Now she could hear someone breathing in short raspy, nervous breaths.

"I'm not going to bother you," she said distinctly. "I just need to find my way—"

Something cold and thin wrapped around her throat. It tightened quickly, cutting into her tender flesh like a wire through soft cheese. Struggling to pull air into her lungs, Jennifer choked and coughed.

Flailing wildly with her arms, she tried to push her attacker away from her. Her grasping fingers tangled in clothing, pressing back against the body inside. Sadly, her enemy was much stronger. It didn't take long. She grew weaker by the second. Her body felt as if it were collapsing like a leaking balloon. Her lungs screamed for oxygen.

Clawing at the brittle noose but unable to force her fingers between it and her flesh, so deeply had it cut in, Jennifer fell to her knees. The noose tightened one final notch. Her hands fell limply to her sides, and she slipped the remaining few inches to the ground.

Jennifer sensed rather than saw the light go on. Only a distant orange glow pierced her closed eyelids. Voices . . . there were voices again in the distance . . . so far away she could barely make them out.

The last sounds I'll ever hear, she thought sadly.

Troy Black helped an attendant roll the stretcher toward the ambulance. Just as he braced himself to lift, a photographer from the *McCarter News* flashed a bulb in his face.

"Know who she is?" the guy asked between shots.

"Check with the sheriff's office in the morning," Troy said bluntly. "Her folks have to be notified first."

Feeling incredibly nauseous, Troy climbed into the back of the vehicle with the attendant and listened as the driver radioed ahead to the county hospital.

"This one might be D.O.A. before we can bring her in. She's unconscious, weak heartbeat. Over."

Troy sat on a low metal stool beside the stretcher and stared at the ashen face of the girl as the ambulance sped off across the parking lot, its siren screeching. She was pretty and much too young to die. Long black hair. Ebony eyelashes that curled down over colorless cheeks. Her eyes were an unusual violet-blue. Cornflower, his mother used to call that shade. Of course, now he couldn't see them. But he'd noticed them a dozen times since he'd started working at the mall.

He swore aloud, and the ambulance attendant, a young Mexican-American, looked at him. "She a friend of yours, man?"

"No . . . yes, in a way," Troy admitted. He would have liked to know her better. Touching the sleeve of her white cotton blouse, he noticed how blood from the circular wound around her throat had spattered a gory pattern over the fabric. "It's my fault that this happened," he whispered dismally. "I should have gone with her."

"Hey, don't blame yourself. That mall's a pretty big place, and no good to hang out at late at night. I wouldn't."

"Yeah." Troy didn't feel any better. He was shaking inside like an off-balanced washing machine in spin cycle. *Jennifer*, Troy thought, remembering the name tag on her apron. *Such a sweet name.*

The attendant was pressing a stethoscope to the girl's arm above a Velcro blood pressure cuff.

"Blood pressure dropping," he called forward to the driver. "Get the lead out! She's going fast!"

The ambulance flew down the highway, as if death itself were in pursuit.

A moment earlier Troy had felt only remorse. Now anger swelled inside of him until all he could see was a savage red haze. He'd get whoever had done this. He'd get them good!

The ambulance screeched to a stop. Flinging open the doors, the attendant jumped out.

Troy couldn't make himself move. He wanted, somehow, to say good-bye to her . . . to this girl who had done strange things to his heart just by smiling at him from behind the Caramelbun counter . . . to this girl who was dying.

Ignoring the attendant's stare, he bent down and kissed Jennifer lightly on the forehead.

"I'm sorry," he choked out.

Chapter 2

JENNIFER FELT AS if she were floating. It wasn't an entirely pleasant sensation, though. Something was holding her down. Every time she tried to break free, it tugged her back down where she didn't want to be.

However, even her frustrated floating was better than the nothingness that had preceded it. She couldn't remember ever feeling so lonely, so helpless and lost. This was a bleak world with no time, no light, no familiar voice or face to comfort her.

"She's coming around." The words seemed unnaturally distant, the voice unfamiliar.

"Jenny . . . Jen, it's your father. Come on, sweetheart, wake up."

"Don't rush her," the other voice cautioned.

"I'll damn well talk to my daughter any way I like!"

Jennifer smiled. Her father's temper was legend. "Daddy?" she murmured.

Slowly she opened her eyes to see a blurry image of her father's gaunt face looming over her. He grasped her hand and squeezed it gratefully. Standing beside him was a young woman wearing a stethoscope and an older man she didn't recognize. He wore some kind of uniform, like a military or police officer's.

The stranger moved toward her bed. "Do you feel like talking, young lady?" he asked.

"Not yet, Sheriff," the doctor cautioned him. "Let me have a few minutes alone with Jennifer, gentlemen."

Jennifer gave her father a weak smile to let him know that she'd be okay without him for a little while.

"I'll call your mother," he said, as he backed out the door. "She's at home. Needed some sleep."

As soon as the door closed behind them, Jennifer cautiously turned her head on the pillow to observe the tubes running into her arm from a pair of bottles suspended on a steel frame. She felt incredibly weak, but the urge to roll over onto her stomach, where she always slept, was almost impossible to resist. She looked up at the woman beside her bed.

"Can you take these out?" She hated needles. How long had this one been taped into her wrist?

"Soon," the doctor promised, patting her arm. "First things first. I'm Dr. Bailey, and I need to give you a complete examination."

The woman spent the next fifteen minutes poking Jennifer in every conceivable spot while asking if she felt the pressure or if it hurt. Apparently Jennifer gave all the right answers. The doctor looked pleased.

"Very good. We'll leave the tubes in for the rest of the day. Tomorrow the intravenous can come out and you may try some real food. Considering what you've been through, I think it's wise to take things slowly."

"What I've been through?" Jennifer asked.

"The attack. At the mall." Dr. Bailey looked concerned. "You don't remember?"

"I remember closing up last night. I had to do it alone. Then I walked to my car and . . . No, wait . . . I don't remember actually getting into my car." Jennifer stared at the doctor. "What happened to me?"

"Don't panic. If you recall that much, the rest will most likely come back to you. I should tell you, however, that you weren't at the mall last night. You've been unconscious for nearly a week."

Jennifer swallowed. Her throat felt painfully dry, and

she glanced at the water pitcher beside her bed. The doctor filled a glass and held it for her.

"A week?" she asked between sips.

"You had a very close call, young lady. I can't tell you exactly what happened to you or why, but the result was, your brain was deprived of oxygen. We call that condition anoxia. Without oxygen, the brain temporarily shuts down. If the deprivation continues for more than just a couple minutes, permanent damage results and . . . death." Dr. Bailey smiled encouragingly. "The good news is, you're going to be all right. Just don't expect too much of yourself too soon."

"You said I was attacked?" Jennifer asked weakly. "Do you mean attacked like . . . like raped . . . or attacked like beaten up, or . . ."

"I was here when they brought you in," Dr. Bailey explained solemnly. "There was no evidence of sexual assault. Whoever hurt you must have had another motive. Perhaps robbery. Your purse was open, no money in your wallet. Loy Patterson, our sheriff, has been working on that angle. Do you feel up to speaking with him for five minutes?"

Jennifer nodded, although she wasn't sure what, if anything, she really did feel up to doing. Her head was spinning.

"I'll be checking on a patient next door. Before I go back to my office I'll stop in to make sure you're comfortable."

"Thank you," Jennifer murmured. Attacked? At the mall? She couldn't remember a thing after locking the sliding grate at Caramelbun. Oh yes, there was that security guard. He'd spoken to her.

Thinking about him made her automatically imagine how she must look after spending a week unconscious in a hospital bed. She glanced at the table beside her bed. Someone—her mother probably—had brought her comb, brush, and hand mirror from her dresser at home.

It was a sterling silver set she'd received for her sixteenth birthday. She reached out the hand that was free of tubes and picked up the mirror.

Her reflection gazed back at her—dark hair gently mussed but not overly tangled. Her mother or one of the nurses must have brushed it for her. Her face was scrubbed clean of makeup. Her features appeared somewhat sharper than usual, her eyes a little sunken . . . but they were the same deep violet. All in all, not bad.

Then her glance dropped to her neck, and her eyes widened with curiosity. A soft gauze bandage enclosed her throat.

Angry voices erupted outside of her room. She ignored them, transfixed by the bandage. What did it cover?

Gently she pulled one end of the gauze free and began to unravel it. When the skin was bare, she stared in horror at the vivid red scar encircling her throat. Then the moment of terror returned full force. Someone had tried to strangle her! Someone wanted her dead!

"Daddy!" she croaked out.

Her father burst through the door, the sheriff at his back. "What is it, sweetheart? Are you in pain?"

"This," she said, pointing at her neck.

He looked a little rocky for a moment, and she wished she hadn't been so quick to show him her scar.

"Dear God!" he finally managed to gasp. He turned to Patterson. "What kind of security do you people provide? Some maniac hides out in the mall, assaulting innocent young girls! And what do you do about it? Nothing, so far as I can see!"

The sheriff shook his head. "Mall security is contracted out to a private company. They're good people, very conscientious. But they can't be everywhere at once."

"If they cleared out the indigents and drug peddlers that would be a start!" her father roared.

Jennifer closed her eyes, glad her father's fury was aimed at someone else. He could be a terror if you crossed him, she knew that from experience. But at least this time he was on her side, and she felt thankful.

"Those homeless folks are harmless, Mr. Merrill," the sheriff assured him. "They're just looking for a safe place to spend the night, and—"

"And the pushers?"

"I was just about to say that we have no proof illegal substances are being sold at the mall."

"Bull!" her father roared.

Dr. Bailey stepped into the room wearing a stern expression. She glared at both men. "I agreed to let you speak quietly to Jennifer for five minutes. Fighting over her bed will do her no good. You'll have to leave now."

Her father muttered something about arrogant physicians.

Sheriff Patterson looked sheepish. "I'm sorry, Doc. Mr. Merrill is justifiably upset, but we're doing the best we can. I really need to ask this young lady a few questions."

"It will have to wait until tomorrow," she said firmly.

The sheriff glanced one last time at Jennifer. She didn't say a word. She was glad they were going. She had a lot of thinking to do.

Patricia McMurphy knocked timidly on the front door of the Merrills's house. She shifted an armload of books from one hip to the other and waited patiently. Finally Gloria Merrill opened the door.

"Hello, Patty, come in."

"Is Jennifer awake?"

"Awake?" Mrs. Merrill laughed, then lowered her voice. "It's all I can do to keep her from going to school."

"I wish my mom would say that . . . just once in my lifetime," Patty said wistfully.

"Well, I wouldn't wish that on you or anyone else." Mrs. Merrill's eyelid twitched, and she blinked several times as if trying to make it stop. "Not if they had to go through what poor Jen did."

Patty had never felt comfortable around Jennifer's mom. She was the kind of woman who fidgeted through PTA meetings if she didn't have knitting to keep her hands busy. When she spoke she never seemed sure of herself. At the end of every sentence she paused as if waiting to be graded on her word choice.

Patty suspected her jittery nature had something to do with her husband. Mr. Merrill was very strict with Jen, hadn't let her date at all until she turned sixteen, and then handpicked her escorts from members of the Merrills's church. Once she and Jen had come home half an hour late from a party and he'd put Jennifer on restriction for two months. Two months!

"He just worries about you," she'd heard Jennifer's mother tell her later. "He doesn't want you getting mixed up with the wrong crowd." The Merrills seemed very class-conscious.

Actually, Patty was surprised her friendship with Jennifer had been allowed to happen at all. Although there were plenty of Spanish-American families living on ranches and in little neighborhoods around the tritown area of McCarter, East McCarter, and Waverly, Texas, there were few black families. When the McMurphys moved from Washington, D.C. to a part of the country reputed to be difficult for minorities, Patty had at first felt a little awkward about the rich chocolate hue of her skin. But she'd been pleasantly surprised when most of the kids at McCarter High welcomed her.

Of course, the fact that her father had recently been appointed chief executive officer of a Houston-based computer company might have made a positive impression on Mr. Merrill. Patty didn't care, as long as she and Jennifer could be friends.

She followed Mrs. Merrill into the living room. "It's okay. I can take myself up to Jen's room," she said. "I'm sure you're busy."

The woman cracked a lopsided smile. "I do have dinner to start," she admitted. "Jen will be happy to see her school books."

At the third door on the right side of the hall, Patty called out, "Knock, knock!"

"Come in!" Jennifer squealed, swinging open the door. "Oh, am I glad to see you! I thought I'd die of boredom. I've read every magazine published in the last six months. *Popular Puzzles* wins hands down for being the most obviously stupid." One look at the impressive stack of textbooks in her friend's arms, though, and her enthusiasm faded. "On second thought, go away."

"Your mother seemed to think you'd be thrilled to see these."

Jennifer rolled her eyes. "They are about the only thing I haven't missed while I've been recuperating. A week in the hospital and another at home. This is just about killing me!" She winced. "I retract that statement."

"Well," Patty said, setting the books down on the night table beside Jennifer's bed, "I don't think the first week counts, since you weren't exactly functioning."

"True," Jennifer sighed, then made a sour face. "I suppose you've very carefully collected assignments from all of my teachers."

"Of course." Patty grinned. "And something else." She pulled out a huge card made from construction paper and pictures clipped from magazines. It said, "We Miss You, Jen. Get better and hurry back to the gang!"

"Everyone signed it?" she asked, amazed.

"The whole junior and senior classes. They all feel pretty bad about what happened to you. I think it hit harder because it made everyone think about last year with Pete."

Jennifer took a deep breath and let it out slowly, thinking about Patty's handsome boyfriend. Pete Foley had been one of Jennifer's teammates on the tennis team, as well as a talented kicker for the Eagles's football squad. He was a smart, athletic young man who'd been super popular. Patty had nursed a crush on him since seventh grade and had just started dating him.

Pete led a truly charmed life: great grades, spectacular wins on the tennis court, the admiration of his classmates. His only problem was his brother Mike, who was one year older. Mike was as bad as Pete was good. He never studied and only passed his courses because Pete wrote his term papers for him and drilled him before every test. He spent most of his time picking fights and drinking with guys five years older than he was. As a consequence he got himself into one tight jam after another. Pete was always there to bail him out.

No one thought Mike would live to see his senior year. But it was Pete's body, with a suicide note pinned to his tennis jacket, that was found hanging from the goalpost on the lower field one autumn morning.

Everyone said it was Mike's fault. Pete just couldn't take any more of his brother's life on the edge.

His death had so shocked his classmates that the school guidance office had been swamped with requests for special counseling, including one from Patty, who'd been hit especially hard by her boyfriend's senseless death.

But Pete had taken his own life, and someone had tried to kill Jennifer. They were two entirely different situations.

"Well," Jennifer said softly, "I'm just fine. In fact, Dr. Bailey says that if I want to I can go back to school on Monday."

"Really?" Patty beamed.

"Yeah. So tell me, what have I missed in two weeks?"

Patty proceeded to fill her in on the latest gossip. A

girl in the junior class was rumored to be pregnant. She'd thrown up three times during the week and Patty was sure she'd started wearing baggy clothes for only one purpose.

Jennifer was unconvinced. "She might have the stomach flu and just happened to have gained weight recently."

"We'll see. If she transfers to another school next month, that'll be a sure sign." McCarter was a very conservative town. No one ever had a baby unless she was married, even if the wedding was a hasty ceremony.

Jennifer shook her head. "What else?"

"Do you know Louise Smith?"

"Short brown hair with a perm and glasses? She works at Books N Things in the mall?"

"The same." A calculating glint lit Patty's dark eyes. "She is hot for Ben Derby."

"No way!" hooted Jennifer.

"It's true. I saw her ogling him at the tennis match yesterday. She hates sports, all she knows is books . . . but she was there in the stands watching."

"Did he take his opponent?"

"Slaughtered the poor guy. Six-three, six-one, six-one."

Jennifer smacked the bed covers with her hand. "Fantastic!"

She wished she'd been there to cheer Ben on. He was a great tennis player.

He also was a hopeless flirt and not to be trusted where women were concerned. It was rumored that he'd had an affair with the young chemistry teacher last year, but she'd left McCarter before anyone could verify the facts. Then there was the divorced Waverly woman with a young child. He'd spent a lot of time last summer in Waverly.

"What else?" Jennifer asked.

"Mall security has started spot checking bags as people leave the stores."

"Does this have anything to do with me? You know . . . because of that night?"

"I don't think so. I suppose they're just trying to clamp down on shoplifters. My manager said there seems to be more of it than usual." Patty's face brightened. "Wait 'till you see the two new outfits I bought . . . well, I've almost bought. They're on layaway. I'll finish paying them off with my next paycheck."

Jennifer laughed. "Don't you ever save any money?"

"Save?" Patty looked perplexed, as if Jennifer had just tossed a foreign word into the conversation.

"You know . . . put some in the bank instead of blowing it all on clothes the minute you get it?"

Patty shrugged. "I will someday. I think I'm a clothesaholic. I just adore cute little outfits with matching accessories and shoes and all. I can't let some gorgeous dress pine away for me on an ugly old mannequin."

"Give me a break."

Patty sighed. "It's a disease. Well, anyway, do you want me to study with you?"

"No." Jennifer paused. "What I really want to do is go back to work."

Patty stared at her. "I don't believe you! After what happened you want to go back to the mall? The police don't even know who did it."

"I realize that." Jennifer stifled a shiver. "My dad wants me to quit. But you know how he is. If I don't have a job, I'll be back on a skimpy allowance. I won't be able to afford to go out weekends, even if he approves of my date. And if I'm not in school or practicing tennis, he'll expect me to be home."

"I see what you mean." Patty said sympathetically. "But do you think your mom and dad will let you?"

"They can't really stop me," Jennifer said. "But, if

I do go back to Caramelbun, I think I'll ask that new security guard to walk me to my car."

Patty's eyes twinkled. "You mean Troy Black?"

"Is that his name?"

"Yeah. I heard someone call him into a store." Patty's eyes flew wide open as she reached into her jeans pocket. "Oh, I forgot something! I brought this to show you."

It was the front page of the issue of the *McCarter News* published on the day following her attack. The headline read: Local Teenager Assaulted in Mall. The smaller print below gave a few details, which Jennifer skimmed over without absorbing. What caught her eye was the grainy photograph of a dark-haired girl on a stretcher. She was being loaded into the back of an ambulance. Standing beside the vehicle and holding the girl's limp hand was Troy. The expression on his face as he gazed down at her was both sorrowful and intense.

"That's me," Jennifer whispered hoarsely, unable to take her eyes off the photo.

"Yeah . . . with your security guard. He's cute. Must be pretty old though. I don't think anyone can work security unless he's twenty-one."

Jennifer giggled. "I don't think that's old!" Without thinking, she reached up to scratch an itch under her chin. But the bandages still enclosed her throat.

Sometimes when she swallowed or turned her head to one side, the scar tissue pulled like a Band-Aid, reminding her how close she'd come to the end of her life. Then she didn't feel quite as brave about going back to work.

"I'll bet whoever did this to me is gone," Jennifer remarked, as if trying to convince herself. "Probably some pervert from out of town, just wandering through."

"Is that what the police say?" Patty asked.

"It's one possibility."

"What about that old lady who was strangled to death? Doesn't what happened to you sound familiar?"

"Like there's a pattern or something? I suppose that's another possibility."

"So if this creep's still loose, he could strike again."

"Yeah, I guess so," Jennifer agreed uneasily. Suddenly she felt very cold, as if someone had opened a window behind her back on a winter day. "Let's not talk about this anymore, okay?"

"Sure," Patty agreed, sorry she'd brought up that night. "Let's talk about Maryanne Anderson."

"What about her?"

"I'm absolutely, positively sure she's pregnant!"

"Geez, Patty, give it a rest!"

The following Monday, after a weekend spent reassuring her parents that she had fully recovered, Jennifer returned to school. Although October in east Texas wasn't normally very cold, she wore a turtleneck jersey with her jeans. She felt self-conscious about the scar around her throat and didn't want people to stare.

It felt good to be back with her friends. But she couldn't help remembering that McCarter High students made up more than half of the work force at the mall. And she wondered if her attacker might after all be someone she knew.

It was an awful thought that cast a black cloud of distrust across her day. Jennifer concentrated on her classes, trying to ignore the morbid suspicions that kept hounding her.

As a senior she had the option of taking an easy selection of courses, because she'd completed all of her credits required for graduation. But her father had insisted she make the best possible use of her last year before college. She'd been accepted at three schools: the University of Texas at Austin, Baylor, and Rice. She hadn't made her final decision, but her father was definitely pushing for his alma mater, Baylor University.

First period, she had Comparative Literature, second was Calculus II, third Historical Perspectives (a fancy name for an advanced Texas history class). After lunch, she dozed off twice during French III, then woke up for Tennis Team Drill and finished the day with sixth period Physics: Independent Studies—which meant the students played around with computer programs, designed model bridges and paper clip-tossing catapults, or lounged around the library. It was her favorite class.

Not until the school day was over did Jennifer decide she would drive to Caramelbun to make sure her boss had scheduled her for work sometime during the week. Even though it was daylight and she should have felt safe, walking through the tall glass doors into the mall was the hardest thing she'd ever had to do. She felt as if she were returning to meet death. A terrible chill crept through her nerves and stayed with her as she walked between stores.

The mall was quiet, even for a Monday. Jennifer wondered if news of her attack had driven off customers. She walked slowly along the wide corridor that linked seventy-five shops, past Books N Things, then Happy Feet. Before she reached the food court there was an elevator, which had always seemed to her a rather stupid idea since it could rise or descend only one floor. Then came the bakery and two dozen fast food stands that smelled fragrantly of fried chicken, hamburgers, pizza, and sugary sweet caramel.

Feeling a little more confident, she walked over to Caramelbun. Jerry, rolling out a huge wad of dough, looked up and did a double take.

"Hey, Jen! Good to see you! What are you doing here?"

"Reporting for duty," she said solemnly.

His smile wavered. "You don't have to do that. No one expects you to come in."

"I want to work. I can't stand lying around the house any more."

He laughed at her. "Not many of my kids say that. In fact," he scratched his head, "can't say as any ever have."

"Please, Jerry." If she didn't come back now, she was afraid she never would.

"All right. But not tonight, I'm fully staffed. How's tomorrow, right after school?"

"I have tennis."

"After that?"

She smiled dimly. "I'll be here."

Feeling better now that she'd started to restore her normal routine, Jennifer spent the next hour window shopping, then dropped in on Patty at Maxie's.

Patty wasted no time before pointing out the latest arrivals. "I have my eye on that red sequined gown," she said after they'd checked out the whole department. "It would be perfect for Homecoming."

Jennifer turned over the price tag. "Two hundred fifty dollars!" she choked out.

Patty winced. "Well, almost perfect."

"Cheer up . . . maybe it will go on sale."

"Maybe," Patty repeated thoughtfully. "Listen, I gotta get back to work. See ya at school tomorrow."

"Sure." Jennifer left to check on a new CD she wanted. She peeked cautiously into SuperCharged, hoping her father wouldn't be around. Gary Pyzik, his assistant manager, stood alone behind the cash register. When he'd finished with his customer, she asked him about the recording she wanted.

"Sorry, Jennifer," Gary said. *"True Blues* sold out the first week it came in."

"Will you get more in?" she asked.

"They're on order. Should I put you on the waiting list?"

"Sure, why not."

By the time she stood in front of Pizzamania, trying to decide between a slice of thin-crust pepperoni or thick-crust with everything, she felt almost back to her old self. She'd stopped studying every person who passed her as if they were a potential murderer, and her knees seemed sturdier.

Then someone tapped her on the shoulder.

Jennifer swung around, looked up, and stared into soft gray eyes under a thatch of blond hair.

Chapter 3

"Hi! How ARE you?" Troy asked.

"Okay," Jennifer replied. She liked the way he smiled, sort of lazy, with his eyes half closed as if a circus parade could pass in front of him and he wouldn't notice . . . or as though he were on the verge of taking a nap. But behind the half-shut lids and easy smile, she sensed there was strong interest and a lot of thinking going on.

"I'm Troy Black." He turned to show her the McCarter Mall Security patch on his sleeve. "I work here."

"I know," she said. "You were the one who found me, weren't you? You know, when I was hurt a couple weeks ago."

"Why do you think that?" he asked.

"I saw the newspaper photo and sort of figured it out." She'd kept the clipping folded up in her wallet and took it out sometimes to study the two faces in it—hers and Troy's. He looked cautious now, as if she'd discovered something about him he hadn't wanted her to know. "And then there's the sheriff," she added.

"What about him?"

"Well, he must have dropped in at my house every day for a week after I snapped out of loo-loo land." She laughed nervously. "He kept asking me questions about what happened, hoping I'd remember something. Like who did it?"

"Do you remember?" Troy asked.

"I never saw the guy's face."

"Guy?"

"Well, I assume it was a man. Whoever it was was taller than me and pretty strong."

He looked amused. "A lot of people are taller than you, including a lot of women. What are you, five four?"

"Almost. Five three and a half," Jennifer admitted.

"Could have as easily been a woman," he mused.

"I don't suppose you saw anyone nearby when you discovered me lying there."

Troy shook his head then hesitated before going on. "Actually, I didn't find you. Someone called 911. Said a girl had been injured at the mall and told the operator where to find you."

Jennifer thought about this. "Then you followed the ambulance attendants?"

"Right." He seemed uncomfortable with the topic and changed the subject. "Are you hungry?"

"Starving," she admitted.

"My treat, then. Thick crust okay?"

She nodded, glad he'd made up her mind for her. They took their pizza and sodas to one of the little round metal tables in the food court.

"I'm coming back to work," she commented as she licked melted cheese from her fingers.

Troy looked surprised. "Really?"

"Tomorrow . . . probably. I take it you don't think I should?"

"I think it would be smarter to wait until someone finds the jerk who jumped you."

"You think he . . . or she is still around?"

"Once is a fluke. Twice in less than a year is a pattern."

Jennifer nodded, sensing he was right but not wanting to dwell on dark thoughts. She changed the subject.

"Is being a security guard what you do all the time? Like it's your career?" she asked.

"Yes," he replied quickly. "Now."

"What about before?" She took a bite of pizza, watching him curiously.

"Before I joined mall security two months ago, I was in college," he stated shortly.

"Really? Why did you drop out?"

He shrugged. "I guess sitting in a classroom isn't my thing. I went to please my parents and hung on for two years. Eventually I decided I needed something different."

Jennifer wondered if that was all there was to it. She imagined all sorts of dramatic possibilities. He'd left school to find adventure, to escape the pain of a broken love affair, to start his own business, which had gone bankrupt after one year, and now all he could find was a crummy security guard job.

"I'd better get back to work," Troy said, standing up abruptly as soon as he'd finished his half of the pizza.

Jennifer resisted the impulse to pull him back down into the chair and keep on talking. Instead she just smiled at Troy, hoping he'd get the message that she wanted to see more of him. However, he didn't seem to notice her. He was watching the crowd of shoppers, most of whom were drifting toward the exit as the dinner hour approached.

She followed his steady gaze to a thin young man dressed in black leather pants, shiny ebony boots and a stylishly oversized sharkskin jacket that was just a shade darker than his coffee-colored complexion. Mike Foley. Trouble.

Her hand snapped out to touch Troy on the arm. "Be careful," she murmured.

His gray eyes swung back to her for an instant. "I will. You do the same. See ya round."

Her heart took a triumphant swing at an invisible tennis ball and sent it flying into a blue, cloudless sky. *See ya round!* He wanted to see her again, which meant that he liked her! She couldn't wait to tell Patty.

Troy jogged through the crowd, trying to close the gap between him and Mike Foley. He'd been dogging the guy for weeks, but he still hadn't been able to catch him making an actual sale. Watching the guy chat up the kids who hung out at the video arcade chewed at his guts. He himself might not be an angel. But, in his book, anyone who sold dope to little kids was pure slime.

As the hour hand on the mall clock moved closer to six and the crowd really began to thin out, Troy stood in the entrance to the arcade and watched Mike with growing frustration. Talk, talk, talk . . . that was all he ever seemed to do! He must have some way of dropping off the stuff and picking up his money.

At last Troy couldn't stand it any longer. He walked over casually, leaned against the *Arm Wrestle the Hulk* game, and glared openly at Mike.

"Why don't you clear out, Foley," he advised in a low voice.

The boy's dark face tightened into a sneer. "Cause I don't want to, man. It's a free country."

"It won't be free for you if you keep it up. Selling junk to little kids could get you dead."

Mike observed him coldly. "A lot of things get you dead . . . some of 'em not your fault."

"You think I'll feel sorry for you because of your brother?"

"I don't think nothin', man. Just get off my back." The boy turned away.

Troy couldn't contain himself any longer. He grabbed Mike by the arm and spun him around. People hanging out around the arcade made a hasty retreat and passersby steered a wide path around them.

"I mean it!" Troy growled. "Find somewhere else to peddle your stuff."

Mike stared at him defiantly. "I was leavin' anyway. Quit hassling me, man!" He shook himself free and stalked off between the shops, a cocky grin returning to his face as he greeted young people leaving by the same door.

On impulse, Troy's right hand flashed up toward his chest. But in the two seconds it took him to consider slipping his hand inside his shirt, he cooled down and reason returned.

No, he couldn't let Foley jerk him around . . . or make him do something crazy. One bad move could jeopardize everything he'd worked so hard for. He had to remember why he'd come to McCarter.

Immediately, he thought of Jennifer, for she was part of it. The muscles in his limbs lengthened and relaxed as he recalled her smile. He'd been so glad to see her strolling around, looking almost normal. Almost, because a frightened light had twice flickered in her eyes when she'd mentioned that night.

He could tell that she liked him—but he reminded himself that this was probably just the ordinary crush girls got on guys who wore uniforms. Anyway, he couldn't afford to get involved with her. He promised himself right then not to share any more pizza with her, to avoid her if at all possible, and definitely not to ask her out. Too much was at stake to let some high school girl mess with his heart and hormones . . . even if she did have gorgeous eyes.

The next day after school, Jennifer walked out to her car to get her tennis gear for practice. Patty was leaving for the mall.

"I'm scheduled to work three to eight tonight," Patty told her. "Want to have dinner together?"

"Sure. I'll take my break at six."

"Great."

Patty pulled open her car door with considerable effort. She drove a well-worn 1970 VW bug. It had belonged to her father when it was new, then was passed down to her older brother. When he'd gone away to college Patty had inherited it.

"It drives like it's about to fall apart in the middle of the road, but I don't know what I'd do without it," Patty once told her. "I could never save up to buy a car of my own. Affording the insurance is bad enough."

"If you didn't blow all your money on clothes—" Jennifer began speech number three.

"I know . . . I know . . . But when I see something yummy hanging on a rack, I can't resist. What can I say?"

Jennifer had a thing about money. Although her parents were pretty well off by McCarter standards, she hated asking her father for spending money. She put half of every paycheck in a savings account she called her No-Touch. Half of the remaining cash went into her checking account for expenses—like her phone bill (because she wanted her own line), clothes, upkeep and insurance for her car, and the loan payments. The rest was pocket money, which she doled out cautiously for meals at the mall, school lunches, gas, and occasionally a movie.

A year ago, she'd bought herself an adorable Miata convertible—cherry red, with stainless steel wire spokes, imitation leather seats, and a stereo tape player. Her car was her one luxury, and she loved it all the more because she was paying for it all by herself.

Patty broke into her musing. "I met a new guy," she announced, smiling mysteriously at Jennifer.

"Really?" Patty was a hard luck case where boys were concerned. Except for Pete, she never seemed to pick winners. Jennifer figured her clothes fetish was a direct result of sexual frustration. "Who is he?"

Patty hummed a couple bars of a new radio tune. "O-o-o-oh, I think I'll keep that for a surprise. If he shows up tonight at the mall, I'll point him out."

Jennifer grinned. "I can't wait."

She waved Patty off then headed for the girls' locker room where she changed into her tennis whites—a short-sleeved, collared jersey with the McCarter eagle over her left breast, a tiny tennis skirt over special underwear that had hidden pockets for balls, and Asics tennis shoes. With her racquet slung under one arm, she headed for the courts behind the Science Wing.

The team was already assembled. Coach Warner began by congratulating them on their last match, while doing his best to temper his praise with caution.

"Just because Waverly High was easy doesn't mean Sam Houston will be. They're ranked number two in the state. We're number ten. That should tell you something, boys and girls."

She hated that boys and girls business. She glanced at Ben Derby, who wrinkled his freckled nose at her to show he agreed. His rusty red hair shone in the strong afternoon sun. He looked like a leprechaun in tennis whites.

"So, let's give it our best shot," Coach continued. "Two more days of practice, that's all we've got. Pair up, and let's go!"

Jennifer warmed up by hitting backhands off the cement wall. She had a strong forehand, but her backhand was wobbly, especially since she'd injured her wrist last summer. Ben walked over to her before she could pair off with one of the other girls.

"Looks like you could use some coaching on that backhand," he commented solemnly.

"Not your kind of coaching, Ben Derby," Jennifer informed him.

"No, really, look—" Before she could object he took the racquet out of her hands. "You need to hit two-handed, like this." He demonstrated. "See, you increase the power and limit the chance of the racquet spinning in your hand. You try it."

She retrieved her racquet. It was a Slazenger Graphite

wide-body, which gave her less weight to swing plus extra hitting surface. Although her racquet had a light fiberglass frame, her thin wrists and insecure grip sometimes resulted in her skying the ball. Pretty embarrassing during a match in front of spectators.

"Like this?" she asked, trying to mimic Ben's grip.

"Almost." He stepped behind her, wrapping his arms around her to clasp his hands over hers on the leather grip. He stood so close that the breeze off the desert couldn't fit between them.

Jennifer cast a dirty look over her shoulder. "Back off, Derby—right *now!*"

"Aw, Jen . . . I'm just showing you how to—"

"Now! Or my right knee makes friends with your crotch!"

"Okay, okay!" He jumped back, holding his palms outstretched innocently. "I was just trying to be helpful."

"Go help someone else," Jennifer suggested firmly, knowing his game only too well.

He looked around the four clay courts and spotted Caroline Newman, a long-legged blond freshman with more enthusiasm than talent for tennis. The one thing she did effectively on the court was bounce. Ben's eyes lit up.

"Behold, yon lass is in need of serious coaching!"

"One of these days, Ben Derby, your hormones are going to get you into deep trouble," Jennifer called after him, unable to keep a straight face. If he weren't such an obvious flirt, he might be dangerous.

He waved her off, and, a couple moments later, she laughed out loud as he started demonstrating the two-handed backhand for his new pupil.

"How's it going, Jenny?"

She turned to find Coach Warner checking her out with sharp eyes that rarely missed a trick.

"Fine."

"Sure you're ready to play so soon?"

She bit her lip and nodded. "I want to. I've already missed one match."

"It's up to you. But I think I should check you out. Are you thinking of switching to a two-handed backhand?"

"It feels awkward."

"Derby isn't without his faults," Coach remarked dryly. "But he might have a point in your case. You could use a little more power and control. Come on, let's work on it."

Jennifer took her stance on one side of the net, knees flexed and ready to propel her in any direction on a second's notice. Both of her hands were in the ready position on the racquet grip, the stringed face extended vertically in front of her.

Coach Warner moved a wire basket of balls to the opposite side. He hit at least thirty balls well to her left, forcing her to return each as a backhand. At last she seemed to get the hang of it.

"Looks good!" he shouted across the net. "Use it from now on. Okay, let's mix it up a little."

He hit flat shots down the line, lobs way over her head that she had to race back to the service line to hit, and cross-court zingers with spin that danced away from her. Jennifer never let a ball past her without putting out her best effort. After fifteen minutes, she was gasping for breath.

"Not bad, Jenny. You're a little slow . . . too much lazing around in bed, I suspect." He winked at her. "Try running a couple laps around the track before you leave today and for the next few afternoons. It'll build up your stamina."

"If it doesn't kill me," she muttered as she staggered off the court.

Chapter 4

THE MALL WAS pretty busy for a Tuesday night. Boys and girls in jeans and T-shirts walked leisurely from store to store, holding hands or with their arms coiled around each other. Mothers pushed little kids in strollers, but not in the numbers that would turn out on Saturday. Men in Western boots scouted out bargains on bright plaid shirts and new Levis while watching the local girls who grazed through racks of dresses marked Sale.

Jennifer thought sales were particularly funny. Working at the mall she'd learned that some stores always had a "sale" on. Their prices never changed, except right before the so-called sale when items were sometimes marked *up,* so that a few days later a red line could be drawn through that price to make the new one look really cheap.

She met Patty in the food court. Her friend was carrying a bulky tote bag in place of her usual shoulder purse.

"Look what I've got!" Patty squealed, opening the top of the bag just wide enough to reveal a glittering patch of red sequins.

"You bought that dress?" Jennifer gasped.

Patty shrugged. "It was too beautiful to leave for anyone else. Besides, it was the last one in my size!" she added quickly when she took in Jennifer's disapproving expression.

"You know you can't afford it."

"I'll manage. Don't be such a spoilsport. Wait until you see it on me."

"Well, from what I saw of it the other day, I'd say it will look super," Jennifer admitted. "But where are you going to wear something like that?"

Patty sat down at a vacant table in the food court and tucked her bag under the table. "To Homecoming, of course."

"Of course?" echoed Jennifer. "You don't even have a date! Does this sound reasonable? You just spent over two hundred dollars on a dress for a dance you don't have a date for!"

"I'll have one," Patty said, tipping her nose in the air.

She looked almost regal, the way Jennifer imagined Cleopatra might have looked when introduced to Caesar. Other girls who didn't know Patty sometimes thought she was a snob, because of that kind of haughty look she put on so well. But she had a very sensitive side too. Since Pete's death she'd only dated two boys, and they had been friends from school who'd felt sorry for her.

Jennifer patted her hand reassuringly. "Of course you'll have a date."

Patty's gaze swerved to meet hers. "I mean it! You don't think I will, but it's true. In fact, I've decided to ask him this weekend."

"You are going to ask a guy?"

"Sure. Why not? If he's too bashful to ask me, why should we both suffer in silence?"

Jennifer mentally ran through McCarter classmates she'd classify as bashful. One was Louise Smith. The other was a boy Patty had once said was too egotistical for his own mother to love.

"Who?" she demanded.

"I told you—I'll point him out later tonight. He'll be around."

Jennifer shook her head, putting Patty's love life out of mind for the moment. She looked around at a dozen fast food signs, trying to decide what to eat. Since she adored Chinese, she decided on an egg roll and order of fried rice. Patty bought a burger with spicy corkscrew fries.

They ate and gossiped and happily lost track of the time. When Jennifer glanced at her watch, she jumped up, gathering together her trash paper. "Oh, my gosh, I gotta go. I'm late."

"There he is!" Patty squealed.

Jennifer spun around to peer into the crowd of shoppers. "Your date? Where? Which one?"

"In that slick black coat," Patty whispered through a nervous smile. "Isn't he gorgeous?"

Jennifer studied the passing people. Her expectant smile faded as she fixed on a boy wearing an outrageously long leather coat, much too heavy for a warm October evening in Texas.

"That's Mike Foley . . . Pete's brother," she said in disbelief.

"I know who he is," Patty responded irritably.

"But he's a pusher."

Patty shrugged. "I think he's just gotten a bum rap."

Jennifer rolled her eyes. "Oh, sure."

Patty watched him with an expression of rapture on her face. "Really. I think he's nice. He just acts tough, to cover up the hurt. Remember how nuts he went right after Pete died?"

Mike had dropped out of school at the beginning of his senior year. He'd refused to believe his brother had killed himself and sworn to get whoever was responsible. But Pete had left a note, leaving no doubt about the cause of his death.

Can't deal with this anymore.

Everyone knew that the only part of his life Pete had trouble with was his brother. These days, his brother mixed with a worse crowd than ever.

Jennifer grabbed Patty by the wrist and swung her around on her chair to face her. "Are you crazy? You can't get mixed up with Mike Foley! Don't you remember how Pete ended up?"

"That wasn't Mike's fault," Patty objected, tears filling her pretty eyes. "And I think it's cruel to talk like that about him."

Jennifer knew there was no reasoning with Patty. When her friend fell for a guy, he could do no wrong in her eyes. Rob a liquor store, mug three old ladies, or swipe a toddler's tricycle . . . she'd find an excuse for him.

"I've got to get back to work," Jennifer said quickly, starting to walk away.

"No, wait!" Patty cried. "Here, take my bag with you."

"Why?"

"Because I don't want to carry it back into the store. Maxie's security always makes such a big deal of riffling through employees' stuff."

"What do you want me to do with it?"

Patty thought for a minute. "Put it in your car. I have to break the news to my mom before I bring it home. I'll get it from you tomorrow."

"Oh, all right." Jennifer took the tote, but she was already so late she didn't want to blow another ten minutes running to her car. When she got back to Caramelbun, she stuffed Patty's bag behind the counter with her own much smaller purse.

She spent the first hour after dinner rolling dough, slathering gooey syrup over the buns, and shoving trays of sweet rolls into the huge oven. When there were enough for the rest of the night, she relieved Jerry at the counter. But no matter how busy things got, she couldn't stop worrying about Patty. If she fell for Mike like she had for his brother, there was bound to be trouble.

Troy made his usual rounds of the mall walkways, shops, and utility passages that connected the stores. He tinkered with a broken door latch and fixed it. He checked out the elevator, which a customer had reported was acting funny. However, he couldn't seem to find anything wrong with it.

Fixing things was a challenge to Troy. He loved making stuff work again. And since Mall Maintenance was shorthanded these days, his handyman work suited his employers just fine.

He paused outside a dress store and observed a convex mirror high up on the wall. Store employees used the mirrors to keep an eye on light-handed customers. But he was watching the salesgirl at the very back of the store.

She wore her chestnut brown hair pulled back into a ponytail and had long, bloodred fingernails. In the past two months, he'd learned to recognize almost everyone who worked in the mall. This girl's name was Carrie.

Looking bored, she strolled over to a rack, pulled down a dress and held it up in front of her. She nodded as if pleased, then looked around as if to see whether she was being watched.

Troy held his breath. Shoplifting was a major problem at the mall. Surprisingly, stores lost more merchandise to personnel than they did to customers. If Carrie took that dress over to the counter and removed the heavy plastic security tag, he could be pretty sure she'd try to sneak the dress out when she left tonight.

He coughed softly.

With an alarmed jump she stuck the dress back on the rack and looked around. Seeing no one, she glanced up at the mirror . . . and met Troy's accusing glare. Carrie dropped her eyes, marched to a table at the front of the store, and started folding sweaters.

Troy decided he'd make himself especially visible tonight at the employee exit. If Carrie knew she was being watched, that might stop her from doing anything stupid. He didn't want to have to arrest her. A police record would mess up her whole future.

But Carrie wasn't the only person he had on his mind tonight.

Troy walked through Maxie's cosmetic and jewelry departments to the north entrance and peered through the glass doors and across the dark parking lot. He waited.

After a while, he could make out two figures moving toward the mall, keeping to the shadows. The gray-haired man and a woman in her thirties appeared every night shortly before closing. The man was gaunt and unshaven with sunken eyes. The woman's arms and legs were rail thin, and her dress hung from her bones as if she were a wire clothes hanger.

Everything he'd heard about them or observed indicated they were harmless, but people sometimes fooled you. He watched them as they edged cautiously between cars, afraid of being chased off. If the pair had no other place to go, they'd be forced to sleep outside on the ground where they'd fall prey to bugs, lizards, and snakes, as well as the harassment of kids and older folks who should know better.

His eyes shifted to a distant end of the paved lot. Parked under a burnt-out halogen lamp was the old station wagon that belonged to the couple who bought beer outside of town and brought it to the mall to sell to kids. The sheriff's men regularly ran them off, but they always came back and were sly enough to rarely get caught making a sale. Troy himself chased them off whenever he caught them at it, but tonight he couldn't afford to leave the mall. He felt danger prickling the air around him, warning him that he'd better stick close.

He turned away from the doors and walked back toward the food court. Behind the cash register at Books N Things, Louise Smith glanced up shyly at him through Coke bottle glasses, then away. She rarely spoke to people unless they were customers, but she seemed bright and very observant. He'd like to catch her alone sometime and ask her about the night Jennifer had been attacked. Louise might have seen something but was too timid to approach the sheriff. He was also curious to find out if she knew anything about the night old Eleanor had died.

Troy stopped, blinking at a brightly lit sign. Surprised to find himself in front of Caramelbun, he wondered if he'd intended to come here all along.

He waited until the two customers at the counter had been served. The only items on the menu at Caramelbun were jumbo and regular buns, coffee, tea, milk, and orange juice. One woman ordered a single jumbo bun and coffee. The man behind her asked for a box of a dozen regulars. "For my wife," he mumbled sheepishly. "She loves those things."

Troy hid a grin. The guy must have weighed three hundred pounds. No wedding band circled his ring finger.

Jennifer rang up the man's order, then, smiling politely, handed him his box. Troy stepped up to the register.

"Can I help y—? Oh." She hesitated and grinned at him.

"Hi," he said, suddenly tongue-tied. "I—uh—I was thinking you might like to take a break . . . we could talk." *This is business. Strictly business*, he reminded himself as he watched the way the glow from the neon tube overhead glinted through her hair.

"I just came back from my dinner break," she told him. "I don't get another tonight."

"Oh, I see." He scuffed the toe of one shoe along the tile counter base. "Well, I want to see you some time, when it's convenient."

She gave him a funny look. "Are you asking me out, Troy?"

"No, I just . . . well, yes, actually." He'd blown it. He couldn't pretend he just wanted to chat without arousing her suspicion. After all, an ordinary security guard wouldn't be tangled up in a murder, like he was. He had to protect himself. "I thought you and I could . . ." *Think fast, man. Come up with something!* ". . . could go to a late movie after work some night."

She looked at him thoughtfully, then smiled. "I'd like that, Troy. How about Saturday? I get off at six."

"Good," he said automatically, backing away. "Good. I'll meet you then . . . right here . . . Saturday."

He was ten stores away from her before he swore out loud, causing people nearby to turn to see what was wrong. *Real smooth, Troy old man! Real smooth. You've just made a date with the one girl you should keep at arm's length. You don't want her to get mixed up in this any more than she already is.*

He'd have to find some way of breaking their date.

Louise Smith stuck a bookmark between the pages of a paperback entitled *How to Feed Your Lawn* and stuffed it into a slim white paper bag.

"That will be six dollars and forty-five cents," she said to the middle-aged man in front of her. He was almost completely bald.

The man handed her the correct change, and she thanked him. A wicked thought crossed her mind. *Poor guy ought to have bought a book about growing some-*

thing on top of his head instead of in his yard. She giggled to herself.

No other customers were ready to make a purchase, but plenty were browsing through shelves. She stepped out from behind the counter and walked toward the front of the store.

For several minutes she rearranged the displays of bestsellers. People were snapping up mysteries and cookbooks like crazy this month. But the hottest book was a Hollywood actress's unauthorized biography, which had hit number one on the *Houston Chronicle*'s best-seller list.

She'd read parts of the book and decided most of it must have been made up. No woman could have had *that* many lovers in one lifetime!

Chewing her lip, Louise gazed down at the eye-catching purple-and-gold cover. The beautiful blond actress posed in a slinky white satin dress.

Could I ever look like that? she wondered. Well, not quite so slutty. But, if she dressed up in something just a little tight, put on makeup, and maybe did something different with her short curly hair . . . just for the fun of it—would guys finally notice her?

Louise sighed. She'd never had a real boyfriend, and here she was seventeen years old! Most girls she knew weren't even virgins any more. Or at least they claimed they weren't. She suspected there must be a lot more girls like her who were sort of scared or just wanted to wait for the right boy. Sometimes, though, waiting was lonely.

Louise turned around to watch shoppers drift past the bookstore. She recognized most of the kids and many of the adults. She'd lived all her life in cozy little East McCarter. There was only one high school, and everyone knew everyone else.

Her glance drifted across a sea of laughing faces and rested on eyes that sparkled a vivid green. The boy's strong shoulders filled out a McCarter Eagles T-shirt. He had bright red hair. Ben Derby.

But he wasn't alone. Ben had an arm around a girl from Waverly High. Another girl trailed beside them, shooting longing glances at Ben. He winked slyly at her, and she giggled.

Louise's blood boiled. *What a sneaky little cheat!* she fumed. Ben had a shining reputation for skirt chasing, both on and off the tennis court. But he seemed to be outdoing himself tonight. Two at once!

In an unguarded moment, Ben's eyes swerved and met with Louise's. She glared at him angrily before spinning away. What was she doing? His love life was none of her business! *Cool down, Lou. Forget about him.*

Moving like a robot, she continued rearranging books.

"Hi-ya!" a voice called out cheerily from behind her.

Louise felt her insides melt. She closed her eyes for a moment, knowing who would be there when she turned around. With a brave effort, she fixed a professional smile on her lips and faced him.

"May I help you?" she asked.

Ben had somehow detached himself from his two playmates. "I thought maybe *I* could help *you*," he suggested smugly.

"Get lost, Derby."

"Aw, no! Really, sweet face." He flashed her a stunning smile. "How about I drive you home from work tonight. You look tired . . . not to mention a little grouchy. We'll have a good time."

"Fat chance," she muttered, swiveling away.

He leaped in front of her and captured her hands in his. "Hey—I'm not trying to pick you up or anything. Is that what you thought?"

She felt oddly disappointed. "You're not?"

"Naw. I just figured since you live on my way and we go to the same school and all, I'd be neighborly."

"What about the two bimbos?" she asked suspiciously. She was *not* getting into the same car with them. If Ben wanted a harem, he could stock it with someone other than her.

"Oh, them?" He chuckled. "I just ran into the Carmichael cousins tonight. We have nothing in common. They're pretty stupid actually."

"Oh? And you're smart?"

"I like a girl with a head on her shoulders . . . not that I'm trying to flatter you or anything . . . God knows I wouldn't try that, you're too intelligent to fall for compliments. But you do have about ten times the brains of most of the girls I date."

Louise didn't know whether to thank him or tell him to go to hell. She frowned, thinking it over, distracted by the way his freckles crept up into the soft, short red strands of hair in front of his ears.

"So? Want a ride home?" he persisted.

Louise snapped out of her trance. "I . . . I have a ride with Carrie Evans. We work the same hours . . . live down the street from each other."

"No problem. I'll just pop down to her shop and tell her not to wait for you tonight."

"Oh, n-no . . . I don't want you to go to so much trouble—" she stammered.

"No trouble at all, sweet face!" Ben was already backing away. "See ya at ten!"

Louise groaned. *Now I've done it. I'm riding home alone in a car with a sex maniac.*

Well, she comforted herself, it's only this one night, one ten-minute drive. She'd be very cool and formal toward Ben, and he'd get the idea she wasn't interested. After all, he had plenty of girls to choose from, why should he want to hang around her?

Strangely, this last thought made her feel a little sad.

Chapter 5

SATURDAY MORNING JENNIFER woke up tingling all over. For the first five seconds after she opened her eyes, she couldn't figure out why she was so excited. Then she threw back the covers, jumped out of bed, and ran to her closet.

Troy!

She had to find something spectacular to wear to work today, because he would be picking her up afterwards! No, she immediately switched her plans. She would change clothes after work. She didn't want to get into his car smelling like stale caramel.

Jennifer chose wheat-colored jeans and a white blouse with pastel flowers embroidered at the cuffs and collar. Rolling them up neatly, she tucked her clothes into a plastic bag along with a clean washcloth and deodorant. For work, she wore her regular jeans and a bright green T-shirt with gold lettering—McCarter Eagles . . . We're Number One!

She'd never figured out what they were number one at. Certainly none of their athletic teams were ranked first in the state, or even the county. Maybe all schools ordered shirts printed up like that. Finding the idea enormously funny, she laughed out loud.

Somehow, everything this morning seemed fun. Her great mood must be due to Troy.

Once Jennifer reached the mall, though, the day seemed to crawl past. She didn't spot Troy at all until after lunch, and then he seemed preoccupied. She took a break at three o'clock and walked around the corner to SuperCharged. Gary, her father's assistant manager, was showing a Sony CD changer to a boy in her physics class. She didn't see her father anywhere around.

"How's it going?" she asked when Gary was free.

He nodded at her solemnly. "Pretty brisk sales today." Poor Gary was always so serious about everything. She couldn't remember him ever showing up at a party. All work, no play—that was him. Her father had hired him three years earlier, when he was just a sophomore. Now he was Assistant Store Manager.

"Gary's a real go-getter," her father had once told her. "Not like most of these teenagers who bounce from one job to another and show up only when they feel like it. He's got ambition!"

"Where's my dad?" Jennifer asked now.

"In the back." He put a hand out to stop her when she turned that way. "I wouldn't go in there now, if I were you."

"Why?"

"He's kind of . . . upset. About last night."

"What happened last night?"

"Sometime before we closed, a customer ripped off two portable CD players and a mess of discs."

"Oh, no!" Jennifer's glance shot toward the storage area behind the door in the rear wall. It led by way of a short tunnel to the loading dock. "Dad must be furious. This is the third theft this month!"

Gary nodded. "I guess all the stores get hit now and then."

"Not like this." She considered her options. "I'd better talk to him anyway. He left this morning before I could tell him something important."

Gary shrugged. "It's your neck . . . oh!" He blinked, looking horrified. "Sorry."

"No problem." But his innocent comment took its

toll on her nerves. She couldn't forget how close she'd come to her last breath just a couple weeks earlier. It had happened not far from here.

Jennifer walked down an aisle lined with TVs, trying not to think of that night.

Her father's store was the best source of sound and video equipment outside of Houston. Every kid in the school wanted a CD system or wide-screen TV from SuperCharged, but few could afford them. They usually settled for less expensive sport cassette players and boom boxes.

"Dad?" she called softly, poking her head through the doorway.

Her father was bent over a ledger on his desk. His hair was as straight and as black as hers. It had started to recede around his forehead, and he'd put on a few pounds. But he got up at six every morning to run five miles before leaving for the store. He looked younger than most of her friends' parents.

Looking up sharply as she approached his desk, he asked, "What is it, Jennifer?"

"I know this may be a bad time, but I didn't tell you this morning that I won't be coming right home after work tonight."

He turned back to his ledger. "Going over Patty's for the evening? Be home by ten."

"No, not Patty's. I'm going out."

He frowned without looking up. "Oh? Who's the boy?"

Her father had already checked out eight boys at McCarter and given only two his seal of approval. Her other dates she'd had to break.

Nervously, Jennifer ran her tongue along the backs of her teeth. "His name is Troy Black. He works as a security guard at the mall. You've probably seen him around."

"A security guard? You mean he's out of high school?"

"I suppose so . . . yes."

"I think they have to be twenty-one to work security."

"I don't know. To be honest, I hadn't thought about it," she admitted. "He's just a nice guy."

Her father slammed his ledger closed. "A nice guy who does a lousy job of protecting honest citizens!" he growled.

"What?" Jennifer was shocked by his sudden outburst of bitterness.

"I don't know what Mall Management pays these so-called guards, but it's too much! My daughter was attacked on her way to her car, and these sticky-fingered kids are still robbing me blind!"

"Daddy, that isn't Troy's fault!"

"Oh, no? Well, whose fault is it?" He took in the confused expression on her face, and his dark eyes softened. "Sorry, sweetheart, guess I'm taking it out on you. It's just so damn upsetting. I don't want to think what might have happened to you that night if . . ." He shook the memory away. "And I'm taking a terrible loss because of all this merchandise walking off."

"Doesn't your insurance cover it?" she asked quietly.

"Well, of course, some of it. But eventually my premiums will go up because of this. I'm sorry . . . we were talking about your date." He opened the ledger again and instantly became engrossed in the figures. "Tell Mr. Black thank you, but you won't be going out with him."

"What?" she gasped.

"I don't think you should be dating a boy—a man, actually—who is so much older than you."

"Three years isn't very much," she objected.

He checked off four items. "Sweetheart, three years at your tender age is a great deal. He's a working man, been around no doubt, and has had . . ." he searched for a word, ". . . experiences. I feel much better about your seeing boys your own age who have college and respectable careers in their future. Most men employed here as guards are drifters or unemployed ranch hands who are looking to pick up a little easy money."

Jennifer's mouth hung open in disappointment. At last she found her voice. "You're saying you don't want me to see him at all?"

"That's right." He looked up at her for the first time in minutes. His lips were set in a determined line. "Now, I need to get back to work, and so do you. I'll see you at home tonight."

Jennifer walked back to Caramelbun in a grim mood. For various reasons her father had vetoed other dates. She'd been disappointed but had honored his wishes. At the time there had seemed nothing else to do, because he was her father and, in their family, that made him the law.

But this time felt somehow different. She was sure he was taking out his frustrations with the mall security system by refusing to let her date Troy. And that wasn't fair.

She didn't utter three words in the next few hours. Looking worried, Jerry asked if she was sick.

"I'm fine," she told him. But her frustration and anger built all afternoon. By five o'clock she was determined not to back out of her date with Troy.

"Can I cut out for five minutes?" she asked Jerry. "I have to run an important errand."

"I think we can hold out for that long," he agreed good-naturedly.

Jennifer dashed straight to Maxie's. Patty usually worked the Junior Department. She found her clearing clothes out of dressing rooms.

"These girls are absolute pigs!" Patty complained.

"They try on stuff and just throw it on the floor when they're done. I hate to think what their bedrooms look like!"

"You sound like my mother," Jennifer said with an affectionate smile. "Listen, I've got a favor to ask."

"Shoot."

"If either of my parents calls your house tonight, tell them I fell asleep watching a movie with you and I'll be home as soon as you can wake me up."

"Huh?"

Jennifer lowered her voice, as if her father's spies might be lurking in one of the dressing stalls. "My dad says I can't go out with Troy."

"Ooooh, that's awful . . . but you're going anyway?"

"Right," Jennifer pronounced between gritted teeth. "Troy is a nice guy. Just because he isn't in college shouldn't mean we can't be friends."

Patty's eyes widened with concern. "You're a lot braver than me. If my dad had your father's temper, I don't think I'd risk crossing him for any guy."

"Not even Mike Foley?" Jennifer teased.

Patty felt her cheeks burn. "Well, maybe."

Jennifer stopped at the pay phone on her way back to Caramelbun. She dropped in a quarter and dialed her home number. When her father's voice came on the answering machine she waited for the beep.

"Hi, Mom and Dad, this is Jen!" she said cheerily. "Just wanted to let you know I'll be at Patty's house watching a couple videotapes. I'll be home by twelve."

Having made her decision, Jennifer put her father out of her mind. She was going to relax and have fun with Troy. That was all there was to it.

When six o'clock rolled around, she hung her red apron on a hook, said good-bye to the late crew, and took her plastic bag into the ladies room to change clothes. Coming out a few minutes later, she felt fresh from the quick washup and the perfume she'd squirted behind her ears and at the base of her throat. She looked up and down the walkway with an expectant smile, trying to spot Troy in the crowd, wondering if he'd still be in uniform or was a little late himself because he'd wanted to change too.

After another fifteen minutes she moved down to stand near the fountain in the middle of the courtyard. This way she could see further in both directions and more easily be seen. She checked her watch. 6:24. Still no sign of Troy.

Thinking back over the day, she recalled him walking past Caramelbun not long before her shift ended. She'd waved, but he'd seemed preoccupied and hadn't returned her wave. Perhaps he had to stay a little longer than usual to finish up some special chore for his boss.

She sat down on the edge of the fountain, her purse and bag with her dirty clothes in her lap, and waited.

By quarter of seven Jennifer finally admitted to herself that she'd been stood up. If Troy had intended to come for her at all, he'd have sent someone with a message to tell her he was going to be late. She took a deep breath, blinked back tears of disappointment, and started walking toward the exit nearest to her car.

Troy had spent all day trying to think of a way to get out of his date with Jennifer. There were too many reasons why he shouldn't be with her, not the least of which was her own safety. He felt as if he were getting close to wrapping up the job he'd come to McCarter to do. But, the further he got, the more dangerous the situation grew for him and anyone close to him.

By six o'clock he decided to make up some excuse for Jennifer. He could say he had a toothache, or needed to stop by his married sister's house to babysit for her two kids. Anything. But his heart wasn't in lying to Jen. He admitted to himself how badly he wanted to be with her. She wasn't just pretty. She was smart and independent, and he admired her guts for coming back here after she'd been hurt so badly. He liked her a lot.

Troy marched past a shoe store, card shop, and a kiosk selling posters of rock singers. He could see Caramelbun up ahead but Jennifer wasn't behind the counter—then something caught his eye: Mike Foley.

As he jogged through the food court, he put everything but his quarry out of his mind. He didn't want to lose Foley in the crowd. It was unusual for him to turn up this early. Troy figured his change in routine must be a sign that something important was about to happen. He couldn't afford to miss this opportunity; he'd just have to catch up with Jennifer later and apologize.

He tailed Mike, not too close and not too far back, for over half an hour as the kid paused in front of store windows and stared at their displays. He didn't go into any of the shops. He seemed to be killing time—waiting for something to happen, or for someone. At last the boy, dressed as usual from head to foot in black, stopped outside of the video arcade and stood impatiently, fists in his pockets, looking around.

Troy eased up behind him. "What are you doing out so early, Dracula?"

Mike flinched in surprise as he spun around. "Hey, man, this is a public place. I gotta right to be here."

Troy watched a couple of middle school kids steer wide around Foley to enter the arcade. They were two of a bunch he'd warned off a few weeks ago. "Stay away from this guy," he'd told them. "He's bad news. Don't talk to him, even if he says he wants to give you something for free."

Now Troy glared at Mike and said in a low voice. "If you sell drugs to these kids, I guarantee I'll catch you. Sooner or later, you'll end up in prison."

"You won't catch me," Mike muttered tightly. " 'Sides, maybe I'm not here for the reason you think."

"Why are you here then?"

"Just talking to some folks about old times," Mike replied. Neither his eyes nor his mouth smiled.

"Want to talk to me?"

"Not 'specially."

"I might surprise you."

"Doubt it. You weren't even in town when they killed my brother."

Troy frowned. "You still think Pete's death wasn't a suicide?"

"I *know* it wasn't," Mike snarled, his eyes throwing dark sparks.

"How? How do you know?"

Mike shrugged, scrutinizing a couple of passersby. "He was my brother. We knew everything about each other. He wouldn't hurt a fly. And he wouldn't have hurt himself either."

Troy observed the tough-looking boy and thought he saw a flicker of pain beneath the cool exterior. Minutes passed in silence. At last, he lowered his voice. "Listen, I might know something about how your brother died."

Mike whipped around to face him. *"What?"* he demanded.

"Chill out, man," Troy whispered. "I said I *might* know. But I have to be sure first. Stay away from the mall for a couple weeks, let me ask around. I'll get back to you."

Mike glared at him. "Who *are* you?"

"No one," Troy snapped, afraid he'd already said too much. "Just a security guard."

"No." Mike studied him intently. "There's something about you that's no rinky-dink mall flunky. Maybe," he continued grimly, "maybe you were one of those who strung up my little brother."

"I didn't do anything to hurt Pete."

"Prove it," Mike growled beneath his breath.

"I can't." Troy firmly looped an arm across Mike's

shoulders. To anyone watching them, they'd look like the best of buddies. But the threat in Troy's deep voice was unmistakable. "Do yourself a favor, man. Lay low for a while. Things are going to get a lot hotter before they cool down. Your mom can't afford to lose *two* sons."

Mike scowled at him, then roughly shrugged off his arm. "You can't scare me!"

"Maybe I'm just offering friendly advice," Troy said evenly. "Now, move along or I'll find some excuse for kicking your butt out of this mall."

Jennifer stomped down one wing of the mall, took a sharp left, and stepped onto the elevator which took her up to the second level. As she passed Burger Delite, where Ben Derby worked, and Sports Galore, she caught sight of Troy in front of the arcade.

He was talking with Mike Foley, and they looked as if they were having a grand time. She stopped dead in the middle of the walkway. Someone crashed into her from behind.

"Excuse me," she blurted out automatically. She couldn't believe what she was seeing! Troy was so busy hanging out with another guy he'd completely forgotten about their date!

She'd kill him.

In the next moment Mike moved off toward the exit. Troy stood watching him, and Jennifer closed in on her victim with lightning speed.

"Well, I hope you two had a jolly time. I sure haven't!"

"Huh?" Startled, Troy swung around to face her. "Oh, Jen . . . hi! I was just about to—"

"Come pick me up for our date?" she finished for him. "Well, you're over an hour late. I don't like being taken for granted!" She spun away.

Jamming her shoulder against a door at the end of the

corridor, she let herself out into the desert air. Even on an October evening, the temperature hovered close to eighty degrees. The air-conditioning filtered out of her hair and clothes, and she instantly felt steamy. Reaching into her purse, she pulled out her car keys and stuck one into the door.

A hand covered hers. "Wait. Let me explain," Troy pleaded from over her shoulder.

"There's nothing to explain," she answered coolly. "I wasn't important enough to remember. No problem."

"It's not that, Jen." He placed his hands on her hips and spun her around. Before she realized what he was doing, he'd leaned down and kissed her softly on the lips.

She meant to pull away immediately. Unfortunately, her reflexes didn't seem to be functioning properly. Her limp fingers let her purse and bag of work clothes slip to the ground.

He tastes wonderful, she thought.

Troy moved back a couple inches and looked down into her eyes. "I didn't forget you . . . just the opposite," he said in a low voice. "There are things I can't explain right now. You'll just have to trust me when I say I can't talk about them or see you."

"Are you and Mike friends?" she asked.

"That's one of the things I can't explain."

"Are you staying in McCarter, or moving on after a couple more weeks or months?"

"That's another thing . . ."

Confused, she lifted her hands between them to rest against his chest. Her fingertips touched something hard beneath his shirt.

Quickly, Troy stepped back and warned, "Don't—"

Jennifer's eyes widened. "What's that?" she demanded.

"Nothing."

"It was. I felt something hard, like metal. Is that a gun?"

"Don't be ridiculous. Security guards aren't issued firearms." Sweat beaded his brow. He avoided her eyes.

Jennifer stared at him, an icy chill ripping through her nerves. "It *is* a gun," she whispered.

Without waiting for an explanation, Jennifer pushed Troy aside, swung open her car door, and threw herself inside. She started the motor with a roar and burnt rubber backing out of the parking space.

A lump of fear the size of a caramel roll lodged in her throat and she squealed out of the lot. All the way home she couldn't stop shaking and her brain demanded, *What have I gotten myself into? Oh God, what am I going to do?*

Troy stood behind the mall and watched Jennifer drive away. He was sorry to have scared her. He hadn't intended to. But maybe it was for the best.

He walked over closer to the building, then, after looking around to be sure no one was watching, he stepped behind a cement pilaster. Reaching into the opening of his jacket, he pulled out the dull black .45 automatic and checked to be sure the clip was full before replacing it in his shoulder holster.

Chapter 6

JENNIFER PULLED UP in front of Patty's house, but she didn't get out of the car. Sitting behind the steering wheel, she forced herself to think about what had just happened. Her head spun and she felt totally confused. Troy had seemed like such a nice, down-to-earth kind of guy. Why was he packing a gun?

After about twenty minutes, Patty came out to the car. "Do you mind telling me why you're parked outside my house when you are supposed to be on a date with the love of your life?" she asked sweetly.

"Because the love of my life stood me up," Jennifer snapped.

Patty's expression immediately turned sympathetic. "The rat! Come on inside and we can talk about it. My mom made chocolate chip cookies."

"Great," Jennifer said dryly. "I'll eat two or three dozen. That ought to take the edge off my mood."

They sat at the kitchen table with tall glasses of cold milk and a mountain of cookies on a plate between them. Even at eighteen, practically an adult, Jennifer found nothing more soothing than milk and cookies. She ate the first four in silence, enjoying the taste of the brown sugar and the rich, sweet crunch of the chocolate bits.

At last, she let out a long sigh. "It's actually worse than just being stood up," she admitted.

"What can be worse?" Patty asked, then immediately gasped. "Oh, no—you saw him with another girl."

"No, with a guy."

"Oh, God! How humiliating!" Patty groaned.

Jennifer cast her friend an impatient look. "Not *that* way, dummy. He was talking with Mike Foley."

Patty's eyes sparkled with interest. "Really? Oooh, that's cool. Maybe we could double date?"

"Give it a rest." Jennifer shook her head. "Maybe you refuse to see it, but Mike is dangerous . . . and I'm beginning to think that whatever is going on at the mall, not only is Mike involved, but Troy is too."

"Good old McCarter Mall," Patty mused. "It used to be such a neat place. Now old ladies get knocked off and my best friend is nearly strangled to death—"

"And so much merchandise disappears that my dad's insurance rates are skyrocketing."

Patty shook her head. "They ought to call the place Macabre Mall," she murmured, "with so many spooky things going on there."

"I agree." Then Jennifer took a deep breath and blurted out what was really on her mind, "He was carrying a gun."

Patty's head jerked up. "What? Who was carrying a gun?"

"Troy."

"Honest? You saw it?"

"I didn't actually see it. But it was under his shirt. I could feel the shape of it against his chest."

Patty grinned wickedly and nibbled a cookie. "You were touching his chest?"

"Oh, good grief—" Jennifer sputtered. "No, I wasn't touching his chest . . . not really . . . I just . . . well, after he kissed me, I just reached up to—"

Patty shot up out of her chair. "He *kissed* you!" she hooted.

"Sh—" Jennifer glanced worriedly toward the kitchen door. Mrs. McMurphy was somewhere in the house.

Patty pulled her chair over beside Jennifer's, plopped

down on it, and leaned close to whisper, "He kissed you. That's what you said. Right?"

Jennifer bit her lip. "Yes. And now I think I shouldn't have let him."

"Why? He's a great-looking guy."

"Security guards tote walkie-talkies, not lethal weapons!" Jennifer snapped.

"So, maybe he's afraid of running into trouble. It's for his own protection."

"Does Troy look afraid of anything?"

"No," Patty admitted reluctantly.

Jennifer sighed. "I asked him what he was doing around Mike. He refused to tell me. I asked him if he'd be staying in McCarter for long. He wouldn't answer. I don't know what to do! He's obviously hiding something. Should I go to Sheriff Patterson's office and report that Troy's illegally carrying a firearm? Or should I just ignore it?" Something terrible occurred to her, and she dropped her head into her hands. "Who has the easiest access to the stores, round the clock?"

"I don't know," Patty answered in a tight voice.

"Security guards . . . and they're beyond suspicion. What if shoplifters aren't carrying off all the stuff that's missing? What if Troy and some buddy of his—Mike or someone else with the right contacts to sell stolen stereos—are snatching things at night?"

Patty's face had paled. "I suppose that's possible. But I don't think Mike would—"

"Oh, come on!" Jennifer hissed. "If I can be honest enough to suspect Troy, you can be open-minded about Mike. Besides, look at this—"

Jennifer yanked her purse from beneath the kitchen table and pulled out the newspaper clipping. She pointed at the figure standing beside the stretcher.

"Troy," Patty observed.

"Right. He was there the night I was attacked."

"But, wasn't he the one who called for the ambulance? Didn't he find you?"

"No. He said that the ambulance just showed up. That was the first he knew that anything was wrong. Someone else called anonymously." Glaring at the grainy photo, Jennifer tugged at a strand of black hair. "Troy was somewhere in the mall when it happened."

"What are you saying?" Patty demanded. "That Troy tried to kill you?"

Jennifer chewed her lower lip. "I don't know. It's horrible to suspect him. But . . . but what if he's mixed up in something illegal? What if I just happened to stumble on something incriminating that night . . . and now he wants to date me, just to keep an eye on me."

Patty dunked a cookie in milk over and over again until a chunk fell off and floated. She scooped it out with her fingers and popped it into her mouth. At last she asked, "Do you remember seeing anything strange that night?"

"No. But I might have blanked it out. And if that was why I was strangled, maybe it's the same reason Eleanor Duvall was killed. She saw something that would put someone in jail."

Patty shoved her half-full milk glass and the plate of cookies away. "I've lost my appetite. Murderers in the mall . . ." She glanced at the newspaper clipping again, then at Jennifer. "Troy looks so concerned about you . . . so worried."

"I know," Jennifer agreed softly. "But I can't stop wondering if it's the kind of worry you feel about a person you care about, or the kind of worry when you're afraid they're going to do something to hurt you. Maybe he wanted to make sure I was dead."

They sat staring at one another, eyes wide with fear.

At last, Patty asked in a hoarse voice, "What are you going to do? Go to the sheriff?"

Jennifer shook her head slowly, suddenly unsure of

herself. "Not yet. I don't have any proof . . . just feelings, and one gun."

"So, in the meantime, you'll stay away from Troy. Right?"

"No-o-o-o," Jennifer said slowly. "I think I'm going to ask him out."

Patty nearly fell off of her chair. "What? Are you crazy?"

"Don't worry. Our date will be on my terms, somewhere with lots of people around. Somewhere safe. I won't let him catch me alone again."

"But why? If you're so scared of him . . ."

"I don't know," Jennifer said thoughtfully. "That's the strange part. I'm scared of what I can sense happening all around us, but can't see. Troy's mixed up in it somehow, and I need to find out how. If he attacked me and killed that old lady, maybe I can uncover proof and take it to the sheriff before Troy hurts anyone else. If I'm wrong and he has nothing to do with all of this, I still might turn up a clue to who jumped me. But I can't just run away from Troy—from what happened to me. If I do, I'll be afraid for the rest of my life. I'll never feel safe until the person who attacked me is behind bars."

"You're either crazy or incredibly brave," Patty remarked solemnly.

A half hour later, Patty wished Jennifer good luck and warned her to be careful. She watched her friend drive off in the dark, then went up to her bedroom, intending to study for her history exam on Monday. Instead, Patty lay down on her bed, staring at the ceiling and nervously biting her already chewed-off nails.

It didn't seem fair for Jennifer to dismiss Mike the way she had—just say he was no good. After all, the guy Jennifer liked, Troy Black, was obviously leading her on and keeping some pretty dark secrets from her. A gun—good grief!

It was all very well for Jennifer to say she was going to date Troy just to gather evidence against him. To Patty this seemed like just an excuse to be around Troy.

Well, if Jennifer could snoop around to discover what her boyfriend was up to, why shouldn't she do the same? After all, Mike had been Pete's brother. He couldn't be as bad as people said.

She decided that the next time she saw Mike she'd ask him to Homecoming. With three weeks before the dance, they'd have time to get to know each other better. Feeling warm and hopeful, Patty held up a hand and wiggled her fingers. She might even spring for a manicure before the dance.

Chapter 7

As soon as school let out on Wednesday, the first day she didn't have tennis practice, Jennifer jumped into her car and drove straight to the mall. She was determined to get there early enough to hunt down Troy before she had to report for work.

She hurried through the upper level entrance. Passing the noisy arcade, she glanced inside. Just ten minutes after school let out, and the place was already filling up. She rushed past dozens of other shops, including SuperCharged, where Gary stood behind the desk showing a CD changer to a customer.

Jennifer found Troy standing outside the bookstore, talking to Louise Smith.

Louise looked around with a friendly smile. "Hi, Jenny. Are you working tonight?"

"Yeah. I see you are too," she returned. "Do you stay until closing today?"

"Yes, unfortunately. I don't like being the last one out," Louise admitted. "This place gives me the chills at night. I don't see how you did it . . . came back after that horrible experience."

Jennifer shrugged. "I'm sure our fine security force has run off all the killers by now," she said, casting Troy a wry glance.

He looked away.

"Well," Louise said, glancing back and forth between Jennifer and Troy as if sensing the tension between them, "I'd better get to work. Talk to you later, Troy. You too, Jenny."

She left them standing alone together. Neither Jennifer nor Troy said a thing for a long time.

At last, she murmured, "Louise is a nice girl."

"The best," Troy agreed.

Jennifer coughed softly, working up her courage. She didn't lie very well, but she had to try if she was going to find out anything about Troy. "I, um, want to apologize for Saturday."

"There's nothing to apologize for."

"No . . . really, I mean it. I had no right jumping to conclusions like that . . . accusing you of carrying a gun. That's silly."

Troy took a deep breath and looked as if he were about to say something, but at the last minute changed his mind. "Apology accepted," he said stiffly.

So, she thought, *you're going to lie too.* She didn't for a moment believe she'd been wrong about the gun. Now it was just a matter of discovering why he was carrying it and what he intended to use it for.

"I want to make it up to you," she said sweetly.

"Make what up?"

"Running out on you Saturday night. I'm sure you were looking forward to our date as much as I was."

He studied her eyes, trying to decide if she was serious or teasing him. "I was, Jen," he said softly. "I really was looking forward to it."

Taken by surprise, she blushed and turned her face away quickly, hoping he wouldn't notice. "Well, I just thought to make up for our broken date I'd treat us to a movie. *Lightning Bolt,* that new suspense film, is playing at the Cinema Two." Reasonable-sized cities rated six or more screens at their theaters. McCarter only made it to two.

Troy frowned. "I, um, I don't know, Jen. I'm supposed to work tonight."

"Tomorrow?"

"Tomorrow too," he said slowly, but with a look of regret in his cloudy gray eyes.

"Well," she said, trying to sound patient even though she knew he was avoiding her, "what night *are* you off?"

"Friday," he said after some hesitation, "but I don't think—"

"Great! Friday it is! Do you want to meet me somewhere? No, wait—I have a better idea. I'll pick you up since it's my treat." She grinned at him. *At least that way I'll find out where you live, mystery man.*

"Jennifer, I—"

"Come on," she teased, punching him playfully in the arm. "Where do I come to pick you up?"

"Here," he said quickly. "Here at the mall. I work during the day, but I get off at six. I'll meet you outside the second level entrance."

"Neat! See you later." She backed away, smiling. Hidden behind her, her fingers balled up into triumphant fists. Every nerve in her body tingled with excitement. Or was it fear?

Jennifer arranged with her manager to have Friday off. At exactly 6 P.M. she pulled up in front of the mall to find Troy waiting for her.

Wondering if she was doing the right thing, she leaned across the front seat and unlocked the passenger door.

Troy climbed in. "Nice car," he commented. "Your dad buy it for you?"

She cast him a sideways look. "No. I worked for it. Anything wrong with that?"

Troy shrugged. "Not a thing. Actually, I figured he might be pretty hard up these days."

"Why would you say that?"

"Well, there's all the merchandise he's lost from the store. That's got to cut into his profit margin."

Jennifer shook her head. "I think his insurance covers most of that. He just gets steamed on principle. He can't tolerate a thief; he's the most honest person I know. Once, when I was about five years old, he caught me pinching pennies out of the jar my mother saved to supplement her household allowance. We didn't have much money back then."

"What did he do?"

"Smacked the hell out of my behind with his belt."

"You're kidding!" Troy looked horrified.

"No, he really walloped me good," Jennifer insisted. "I had to eat dinner standing up that night. But you know what? I never took another thing that didn't belong to me. I don't even like asking for money from him now."

"That's why you work?"

"So I can have my own spending money, and a car . . . and get out of the house."

"You don't get along with your parents?" he asked.

She turned down Rio Sancho Street then took the third left into the theater parking lot. "I get along with them as well as any teenager gets along with her parents, I suppose. They're strict but fair. Except where boys are concerned." She glanced sideways at Troy, curious about his sudden interest in her family. "My dad didn't want me to go out with you."

"He didn't?"

In spite of her nervousness, she laughed at his puzzled expression. "Don't take it personally. He vetoes ninety percent of my dates."

"But he sees me at the mall all the time. He knows me, and we seem to get along okay."

Jennifer pulled into a parking space in back of the theater and switched off the engine. "Like I said, don't take it personally. He has this fantasy that I'll go to some elite college, marry the son of a millionaire oilman, then live in Texas for half the year and spend the rest in a villa on the French Riviera where he and my mother can come on vacations."

"He has your future all planned out for you," Troy commented.

"Only he forgot one thing," Jennifer said, opening the door of the Miata and hopping out.

"What?" Troy called over the roof.

"Me. That's just not me," she said.

Inside the theater, Jennifer bought their tickets even though Troy tried to make her let him pay.

"You can buy the popcorn and soda," she told him. "The snacks are so expensive, they'll cost almost as much as the movie."

They took their seats with five minutes to spare before the show started. Jennifer ate a handful of popcorn and looked around the theater seats. A familiar shock of red hair caught her eye.

"Look!" she hissed in Troy's ear. "There's Ben Derby . . . with Louise Smith."

Ben and Louise sat about three rows in front of them. No one could mistake Ben's blazing hair, or his less than subtle approach with girls. Twice, he tried to reach one arm behind Louise and pull her closer. Each time, she leaned away and shook him off.

"They don't seem the most natural couple in the world, do they?" Troy commented, laughing when Louise jabbed Ben in the ribs so hard he bent over double.

"I don't know," Jennifer mused. "Maybe she's what Ben needs. I doubt if he'll be able to charm her into bed like his other girlfriends." She turned to face Troy. "Well, we've talked about my friends and me. Tell me something about you and your family."

Troy shrugged. "We're pretty ordinary. Nothing very interesting."

"Not fair. I told you about mine. Do you have any brothers or sisters?"

"Two brothers," he said gruffly.

"And what are your parents like?"

"They're average parents . . . that's all, nothing exciting. Let's talk about something else."

She could feel tension in his voice, crackling like static electricity. Why wouldn't he talk about himself? She didn't let up.

"Okay, so they're average. Where are you from? Not around here. You came to McCarter just a couple months ago."

He let out a long groan. 'I grew up in Houston. All right? I lived there all my life."

"Really?"

"Yeah." He looked miserable and squirmed in his seat.

Unfortunately, the lights dimmed and the movie started before she could hit him with another question.

The film was exciting, one breathtaking chase scene after another, the kind of movie most boys she knew adored. But Troy seemed distracted. Several times when she glanced sideways to watch his reaction to a scene, she found that he wasn't even looking at the screen.

When the movie was over, he took her hand and started walking silently up the aisle.

"I thought it was good," Jennifer stated as they emerged from the building into the warm night air. "I liked the part when the hero leaped from the top of one building to the next to save his girl."

He grunted.

"Why are you in such a hurry?" She was running to keep up with him as he strode across the parking lot.

"No hurry," he huffed. "Are you hungry?"

"Well, a little, I suppose—"

"Good, I'll buy you a burger at Donovan's. We can leave the car here."

Jennifer glanced ahead in the dark. Several other couples were heading for the popular restaurant—Patty and Mike Foley among them.

Jennifer's stomach clenched in a tight knot. Patty hadn't taken her warning very seriously.

She looked at Troy. His face was rigid, his eyes intently fixed straight ahead—on Mike.

"We're following them, aren't we?" she asked.

"We just happen to be going to the same place," he said tightly. "Come on, before someone beats us to the last table."

Feeling confused, Jennifer rushed on at his side. They arrived out of breath and had to wait for five minutes before being seated a few tables away from Patty and Mike.

Jennifer played with the fake flowers on their table. She felt as if she were spying on her best friend, and that didn't feel right. At last, she couldn't stand it any longer.

"I'm going over to talk to Patty," she announced, and stood up before Troy could stop her.

"Hi!" Jennifer called out above the noise of the restaurant and waved.

Patty squealed when she saw her coming. "Oh, this is fantastic! Hey, you guys, sit here with us!"

Wearing a doubtful expression Troy joined them and sat on the wooden bench beside Jennifer.

The girls decided that each of them should order something different so that they could share. Patty chose nachos heaped with melted cheese and jalapeno peppers. Jennifer asked the waitress for crisp, fried potato skins. Troy ordered a Mega-Burger, with everything. And after long consideration, Mike selected spicy buffalo wings. The waitress brought a pitcher of soda and four chilled glass mugs with the food.

While they ate, the two girls chatted about school. Mike seemed to pay little attention to the conversation, but Troy was surprisingly interested in all of the extracurricular activities and asked a lot of questions about the kids who participated in them.

"We have the usual sports—football, basketball, soccer, field hockey . . ." Jennifer explained, munching on a nacho chip.

"And some that aren't so usual," Patty added proudly. "Not every school has a tennis team or wrestling squad, but we do!"

"Were you involved in any sports before you left McCarter High, Mike?" Troy asked casually.

Mike's dark eyes swerved suspiciously to meet the other boy's. "My brother played some tennis—and he and I were on the football team. He kicked, I was a wide receiver."

"Were you guys any good?"

"The best," Mike answered in a clipped voice.

Jennifer jabbed Troy under the table. What was he trying to do, upset Mike? She couldn't understand why he was being so insensitive. Mike obviously didn't want to talk about his dead brother.

Troy ignored her warning. "A kicker," he mused aloud. "I'll bet a lot of guys would like to get that job. All the glory—not much pain."

"What are you getting at, man?" Mike asked, scowling dangerously.

"Nothing . . . just that a lot of guys must have envied your brother. Everything I hear about him points to the fact he was as popular with the students as he was with his teachers, and now you tell me he held a key spot on the football team."

Jennifer put down the chicken wing she'd been nibbling and stared at Troy. "That's enough," she whispered. She could feel the strain between the two boys, and it was making her even more afraid than she'd been when she'd picked Troy up.

Troy ignored her. "If someone wanted something that Pete had, he or she might have been desperate enough to try to get rid of him. Or," he continued slowly, "maybe Pete wasn't as perfect as everyone thought."

Mike rocketed out of his seat, knocking the table as he stood. The pitcher and glasses tumbled over, and a river of dark soda and ice ran onto the floor. Jennifer stood up, getting out of the way of the syrupy waterfall. Pinned between the table and her bench, Patty sat with her mouth open, looking three shades paler than normal.

"Shut up!" Mike roared. "Pete was a good kid! Better than good—he was great!"

Troy held up both hands in a show of innocence. "Hey, I'm not saying anything bad about your brother. I just thought since you don't believe he killed himself . . ."

Jennifer's ears hummed with the words. *Don't believe he killed himself? Pete?* It was the first time she'd heard anyone question her classmate's suicide. After all, there had been a note. And no one hated Pete. But a lot of people had tangled with Mike's hot temper.

"I *know* he didn't kill himself!" Mike shouted.

By now, everyone in the restaurant had stopped eating and was watching Mike and Troy.

"You . . . know . . . it?" Troy repeated. "Then who did the job, man? Who wasted your brother? Someone who wanted his spot on the team? Or someone who mistook him for *you* in the dark one night?"

Mike's expression froze in a grim mask of horror. Pain filled his dark eyes. He blinked helplessly at Troy, his mouth working but unable to form words.

At last, he regained his voice. "Go to freakin' hell!" he shouted.

Jennifer was shocked. *That's what Mike thinks!* she realized in a flash. *Mike thinks someone was out to get him!* Although there was a year difference in age, the two boys had looked enough alike to pass as twins.

Troy pushed on. "Who was it, Mike? You must have some idea."

Mike shook his head, a cold threat in his eyes warning Troy to stop.

"There is one other possibility," Troy said in a voice so low only those closest could hear. "Brothers sometimes are jealous of one another. They have their disagreements. Did an argument go too far one night, Mike?"

Jennifer tried to step between the two boys, but wasn't fast enough. With a furious bellow, Mike threw himself at Troy.

Patty shrieked and tried to wiggle out from behind the table. Jennifer danced around the two struggling boys. In the next second, they were scrambling on the floor. Mike was on top of Troy's chest, one wide hand clamped across his throat while pummeling him with a knotted fist in the stomach.

Troy winced at the first three blows but, strangely, seemed not to fight back. Then he appeared to get a grip on the situation, wedged a long arm up and around Mike's neck in a headlock and threw him off to one side and onto the floor. In a flash he was on top of Mike, flipping him over onto his belly and pinning his arms behind his back as Mike squirmed helplessly.

Jennifer saw Troy's hand move toward his shirt. *The gun!* she thought wildly. *Oh, God, no!* "Troy don't!" she screamed, launching herself at his back.

He didn't seem to react to her fists pounding on his spine. Reaching inside his breast pocket, Troy pulled out a card and placed it on the floor in front of Mike's bulging eyes.

"If you didn't kill your brother, someone else did," he ground out. "You can't get to them by yourself. Call me when you cool down."

He released Mike and stood up. Grasping Jennifer's hand and dragging her along with him, he walked out of the restaurant.

Jennifer's head spun. She stared at Troy as they crossed the lot to her car. "Who *are* you?" she asked shakily.

He didn't answer. His face was strained with concentration. She wasn't even sure that he knew she was still there.

They got into his car, and only then did he lean forward, drop his face into his palms and groan, "What a mess!"

"I'd say so—" she agreed heartily. "Soda all over the floor, nachos flying, you and Mike wrestling on the floor in the middle of the restaurant!"

Troy sat up straight and glared at her. "That's not what I meant!" he barked.

She shivered at the dangerous edge in his voice. For the first time in her life, she was truly terrified of one of her dates. Headlines flashed through her brain. *Girl Disappears After Date With Local Boy!* Or *Battered Date Rape Victim Appears in Court!*

"You'd better get out," she blurted.

Without a word of objection, Troy opened the door, climbed from the Miata, and started walking away.

Chapter 8

JENNIFER LOCKED HERSELF inside the car and watched Troy plod across the dark parking lot, his shoulders slumped, blond head lowered. He looked as miserable as she felt . . . worse. Taking a deep breath, she forced her hands to stop shaking on the steering wheel. If he'd meant to hurt her, wouldn't he have done something by now? As frightened as she was of him, something inside of her drew her to him.

Praying she was doing the right thing, Jennifer started the car and drove up slowly beside Troy. She cranked down her window.

"Get in," she called. "I'll drop you off at your car."

Making no move to come around to the passenger side, Troy leaned through her window. "I'll walk tonight. I need some fresh air and thinking time." He paused. "Sorry dinner wasn't a little more peaceful."

"I didn't get to eat much, but it was certainly entertaining." She smiled dimly. "I want to see you again, Troy."

His gray eyes darkened sadly. "I don't think that's a good idea, Jen."

"I don't care whether it's a good idea or not, it's the way I feel!"

He considered her pleading expression. "I want to see you too," he said, touching the tips of shiny black hair that fell over her shoulder. "It's just that things are a little complicated right now."

"Oh?" She held her breath, hoping at last for the overdue explanation.

"Yeah, they are," was all he said. Slowly, he bent down and kissed her on the lips. "At this moment, I wish I were anyone but me," he whispered. "Goodbye, Jen. Take care of yourself."

She watched him walk dejectedly away, hands stuffed into his pants pockets. "What is going on in that mind of yours, Troy Black?" she wondered aloud. And why was he ashamed of who he was and what he was doing here in McCarter?

Jennifer sighed. What now?

It was eleven o'clock; her curfew was twelve. She could drive to Patty's house to ask her if Mike was all right. But she didn't dare face her friend so soon after the fight. It would probably be wise to let the dust settle a little.

When Jennifer arrived at her own house, her mother had already gone to bed. Mrs. Merrill rarely waited up for her husband to come home nights, and often was still asleep when he left for the store the next morning.

Jennifer punched the button on the answering machine attached to her phone. There were two hangups followed by a message from Patty, obviously left before their dates:

"Hey, I did it! I'm going out with Mike tonight! Tell you all about it when I get home."

"Don't bother," Jennifer murmured.

She drew a deep breath and let it out slowly. Too tense to sleep, she walked downstairs again and peered into her father's study. He wasn't there, but the light on his answering machine was blinking.

The message was from her father. "Gloria, I'll be home late. We need to finish the stock inventory tonight, and it's taking longer than I'd expected."

Jennifer stood in the dark with her hand resting on the machine. The sound of her father's voice brought on a wave of guilt. She'd lied to him and disobeyed his order not to see Troy.

Although she still resented his meddling in her personal life, she knew she'd been wrong to trick him. There ought to be some way she could make that up to him. She still felt guilty about lying to him, but not guilty enough to confess. However, he must be tired after working all day and half the night. Helping him complete inventory might make her feel better.

Slinging her purse strap over one shoulder, she walked back out the door . . . then stopped, her hand still on the knob. What was she doing? The last time she was at the mall this late, she'd nearly been killed. Tension knotted her stomach, and she wet her suddenly parched lips.

"Oh God!" Jennifer whispered under her breath. "I can't go back there now. Not alone."

But she had to do something to make up for her lie to her father, and she could think of nothing else.

Ten minutes later, her insides tight with fear, she parked beside the loading dock nearest SuperCharged.

Jennifer quickly slid out of the Miata. The parking lot was as dark and lonely as a graveyard. A couple of lights closest to the high cement dock had burnt out. Gary Pyzik's truck was backed up to the ramp, but no one seemed to be around.

Her breath coming in short, anxious gasps, Jennifer ran up the steps and tried the door, but it was locked.

"Damn," she muttered, looking around. The main entrances to the mall would all be secured for the night.

She ran along the wall of the building to the next dock. Its garage-style door was closed off by a high iron gate that folded back like an accordion during the day. It, too, was locked. She returned to the door stenciled SuperCharged and pounded.

"Dad! Dad, are you there? It's me, Jen!"

She kept on pounding, hoping he'd hear her through the heavy metal if he were in the back room.

At last, she heard muffled voices and, slowly, the door cracked open. A pair of eyes appeared in the dark slit.

"Dad?" she asked.

"Jennifer, is that you?" It wasn't her father's voice.

"Gary?" What a scaredy cat he was! Worse than she. But maybe caution was wise. After all, opening doors to strangers at night sometimes proved fatal. "For crying out loud, open up . . . it's creepy out here."

"Hold on a minute while I tell your father that you're here . . . and, um, I gotta move these boxes. They're blocking the door."

"Okay." Jennifer shuffled her feet impatiently while looking around in the dark, anxious to be let in.

It was several minutes more before the door opened. Her father stood beside Gary when she stepped through.

"What are you doing here?" he demanded irritably.

"I came to help," she said. "I heard your message on the machine. I don't have school tomorrow and figured if you didn't have help you might be here all night." She crossed quickly in front of him. "Well, where do I start? With these boxes over here? Got a tally sheet?"

Her father shook his head grimly. "You're not staying. I want you to go straight home."

"Daddy, I'm not a baby anymore! Why are you so hung up on protecting me? I'm okay. I'll be here with you and Gary. When we're done, we can all leave together."

"I said, *you are going home,*" he repeated firmly.

She glared at him. "Not until you give me an explanation," she said.

Her father exchanged a frustrated glance with his assistant, then snapped at him, "Finish up the list in the showroom. I'll be with you in a minute."

"Yes, sir," Gary answered meekly.

Mr. Merrill turned back to face his daughter. Almost

at once his expression softened. "Listen, sweetheart, since your accident, I just don't feel right about your being in this place."

"In your own store?"

"No, in the mall—especially at night. I'm a nervous wreck whenever I know you're working."

She stepped up to her father, put her arms around his neck, and hugged him. "I get scared too." Like right now. "But I want to work, and there aren't many jobs around McCarter except at the mall. I can't shut myself off from my friends or run away from . . . from what happened."

"Has it occurred to you that one of those friends may have been responsible for hurting you? Have you thought about that?" he demanded angrily.

Yes, she had, she admitted to herself with a sick feeling in her stomach. But she hated to believe it.

He gave her a quick squeeze before stepping back. "I just want the best for you, Jennifer . . . and for our town. I can't stomach the thought of thieving, vicious punks destroying a nice place like McCarter."

"I know, Dad."

He looked down at her. "I want you to go home now. I'll have Gary walk you to your car to make sure no one bothers you."

"That's silly, Dad. I'd be with you. You know I'd be safe and—" She broke off, noticing that his expression had already hardened.

Jennifer knew that arguing with him would do no good. Once her father set his mind on anything, he never changed it, never turned back or doubted his decision. She figured that was what had made him such a successful businessman.

Her father called for Gary, who held the rear door open for her. At school some of the kids called him a nerd, because he was always so serious. But she'd never held good grades or a responsible attitude against anyone. She figured he just needed to loosen up a little.

"How's he treating you, Gary?" she asked to make conversation as they stepped out into the night.

He scowled at her. "What do you mean?"

"Nothing in particular. I just know how tough my dad can be. Is he okay to work with?"

"Oh, your father treats me fine. I make good money."

"Well, you should . . . you work hard," she said.

He shrugged.

"Ben told me you have a new computer system."

Gary's eyes lit up. "Yeah, it's super! A Toshiba with an EGA color monitor and laser printer. It's faster than lightning. And the graphics are fantastic."

"Must have cost a bundle."

"I saved up for it," he said, defensively.

"That's how I got my car," she said to put him at ease. "It took me two years of sticking every cent I earned at Caramelbun into the bank to save enough for the down payment. Dad insisted I pay half up front."

"It's a nice car." He stroked the gleaming red hood, his eyes reflecting the blue-white halogen beam from the lamp above.

"Will you be working much longer tonight?" she asked.

Gary hesitated. "No, not much. Maybe an hour and we'll be done."

"Good," she said, starting up her car. She looked around, feeling as if someone were watching them, and a prickly feeling slithered up her spine. Locking the doors, she drove away, glad to be going home. In her rearview mirror she could see Gary opening up the cap on the back of his truck.

Troy walked down the shoulder of the road toward the East End Motel. As he dropped one foot in front of the other, he chewed himself out for being so stupid.

"Great move, dummy! Fighting in the middle of a public restaurant!" What he'd done was totally unprofessional.

And that was exactly what his boss would say the next time he saw him.

It didn't occur to Troy that the man might not find out about his wrestling match with Mike. The guy either saw or heard about everything that happened in Lee County . . . everything except the worst stuff, like who killed Pete Foley and old Eleanor Duvall, and who had roughed up Jennifer. Those were secrets too evil to let slip over coffee at the Silver Diner, or, apparently, even at Jake's Bar over beers.

He shook his head, feeling as if time was running out. But, so far, all he had to go on was a couple homeless vagrants he couldn't catch up with to question, a half-strangled teenage girl who was either too scared to admit seeing anything or simply didn't remember, and the brother of a murder victim whose fuse was so short he was probably useless. In fact, Mike Foley had, to this point, done a fine job of getting in his way.

Troy thought about the boy. He couldn't help feeling sorry for him. If one of his own brothers had been murdered, he'd probably go off the deep end too. Maybe there was another way of handling Mike.

He could take a risk and tell Mike why he'd really come to McCarter. Since the kid was such a loner anyway, he wouldn't be likely to blow his cover.

Troy scratched his head, undecided. On second thought, maybe he should make up some story before enlisting Mike's help. Something to keep the kid in the dark like the others. He'd have to decide which way to go by morning.

Troy walked the last few feet to the motel room door marked *113*. The cramped efficiency had been his home for the last two months. He couldn't wait to get out of the place. He hated motels.

Troy glanced up, then down the row of shadowy doorways and tiny curtained windows before shoving the key into the lock. He turned it carefully, slowly, and edged the door open only two inches before dropping to a squat.

After a few seconds of feeling around on the carpet, he found the telltale scrap of tissue paper he'd left wedged in the door. If anyone had entered the room in his absence—whether they were still here or had come and gone—the paper would have floated into the middle of the room as they walked past. Troy retrieved the little scrap and stepped inside.

He was safe . . . for now. Tomorrow he'd decide how to deal with Mike. Now he had to check in with his boss and get some sleep.

Sitting on the edge of the motel bed, he untied the laces of his tennis shoes with his right hand while punching in the phone number with his left.

When the recorded voice came on the line he said, "This is Weasel. Made contact with Foley and victim number three. No new developments since last report. Expect action tomorrow."

He hung up, laid back on the bed, and, still dressed, fell into a troubled sleep.

When Troy awoke, it was already light. He swore under his breath, tore off his clothes and threw himself into a hot shower. He was supposed to report for duty at the mall at 9 A.M., forty-five minutes before the stores opened. That left him just one hour to retrieve his truck from the mall parking lot and find Mike.

He stopped just long enough at the Silver Diner to pick up a large coffee, then drove on. In front of the Foley house on San Jacinto was a fifteen-year-old muddy blue Chevy. Troy eased his truck past it and stopped at the curb. He took another swallow of the steaming coffee and waited.

At 7:20, Mike ran out of the house. In one motion, Troy set his coffee cup on the dashboard and swung himself out of the truck. He intercepted Mike halfway to the bus stop. Before the kid realized he had company, Troy pinned him roughly against a tree trunk.

"What's your freakin' problem!" Mike shouted. "Hey, let up!"

"We're going for a ride," Troy said calmly, walking him back toward the truck. "Get in and slide over."

"I ain't gonna—"

"Do it or you'll regret it, man! I have something to tell you about Pete."

With the mention of his brother's name, all the fight seeped out of Mike. He climbed docilely into the cab of the truck.

Troy got in after him and started the engine.

"Where are we going?" Mike asked nervously.

"Just around the corner, out of sight of the house. I don't want to alarm your parents and neighbors."

"Oh," Mike said, rolling his eyes, "that explains a lot."

Troy volunteered nothing more until he'd found a vacant lot on the other side of the block. He cut the engine and swiveled around on the seat to face Mike.

"I apologize for last night," he began. "I was out of line. I shouldn't have let you get to me."

Mike scowled at him, but eventually shrugged. "Sometimes I get crazy, thinking of Pete. My little brother was always lookin' out for me, pulling me out of scrapes. The one time he needed me . . . I wasn't there."

"I understand," Troy said evenly. "And I know how bad you want to get the person responsible for his death."

Mike's eyes sparked with interest. "Then you think he didn't kill himself. You agree with me."

"I've known it for a long time," Troy said in a low

voice. He took a deep breath, thinking—*Well, here goes. Truth or lie, which will it be?* "Mike, I can help you get them. I have contacts, and a certain amount of influence."

Mike studied him cautiously. "Mall security guards aren't exactly known for their pull."

"I have friends. Leave it at that."

Mike squinted at him. "Quit jerkin' me around, man. You sound like some mafioso type." He laughed nervously when Troy denied nothing. "How about you show me something to prove your influence."

Troy unzipped his jacket and undid the top two buttons of his shirt. "How about this?"

Mike's eyes widened as he studied the dull ebony metal of the automatic that was strapped to Troy's chest. "Lord, you had that on you last night?"

"Yup."

"You could have wasted me!"

"But I didn't. And I wouldn't, Mike. It's for protection . . . and to let certain folks know that I mean business. My boss wants to find out what's going on in McCarter, and he wants to know fast."

Mike let out a ragged breath. "So you're saying we should team up?"

Troy nodded slowly. "Since you won't back off."

"Tell me what you know so far," Mike said.

"I'm convinced that there's some connection between Pete's death, the murder of that old lady, and possibly with the attack on Jennifer Merrill."

"Wild!" Mike breathed. "But what if I don't agree to work with you?" Mike asked.

"I guess I'd have to find some way to get you out of my way." He intentionally allowed Mike one final glimpse of the gun before closing his jacket.

Mike swallowed. "Guess I don't have much choice, do I?"

Troy shook his head.

Cautiously, Mike held out his right hand, and the two boys shook.

"Where do we start?" Mike asked.

"You go to work as usual. Don't worry," Troy said when Mike looked alarmed, "no one else knows about your job in Houston. I only found out by following you a couple days. For the time being, we'll try to keep things routine and not let people see us together too often. But tonight we have work to do. Meet me at the mall."

Chapter 9

THE DAY DID not start off well for Jennifer.

Since it was Saturday and she wasn't scheduled to work until noon, she'd intended to sleep in. The telephone rang at 8 A.M.

Trying to block out the annoying jangle, Jennifer pulled the pillow over her head, deciding to let the answering machine take a message.

Unfortunately, she had never been able to ignore a ringing phone. *Second ring!* after all, it might be someone terribly important, like a great-looking guy who'd finally worked up enough nerve to call for a date. *Third ring!* And if she didn't answer in person, this very instant, he might be too timid to leave his name . . . and she might never know that he'd called. *Fourth ring!* And for the rest of her life she'd regret—

Her hand zipped out from under the sheets before the machine could click on, and she grabbed the receiver.

"Hello?" she croaked in a sleep-roughened voice.

"Hello yourself, traitor!"

"Patricia? Is that you?" Jennifer sat up in bed, suddenly awake.

"Yes, it's me . . . and I haven't slept a wink all night! How could you let your boyfriend beat up on poor Mike like that?" Patty demanded angrily.

"I didn't have much say in the matter," Jennifer complained. "And he's not my boyfriend."

"You were out with him, weren't you?"

"I'm dating him for a reason . . . to keep an eye on him."

"Oh, sure."

"Come on, don't be mad," Jennifer pleaded. "I'm serious. I told you that I think Troy's somehow involved in whatever's been going on at the mall."

There was a long pause from the other end of the line. "You're serious," Patty whispered at last.

"Definitely. Come on over. I'll make us breakfast and we can talk."

A half hour later, Jennifer had showered and dressed in jeans and her baggiest, most comfy sweatshirt. She was pulling eggs and bacon out of the fridge when a knock sounded at the kitchen door.

"How do you want your eggs?" she asked, letting Patty into the cozy red-and-white room. Curtains, tablecloth, and quilted appliance covers were all sewn from the same brightly checked fabric. Even the plastic strawberry magnets on the fridge matched. Her mother couldn't stand having anything out of order or the wrong color. The whole house was that way—each room perfectly coordinated.

"Scrambled," Patty said.

While Jennifer cooked the eggs and bacon, Patty toasted bread. Before long they sat down to a hot breakfast. Jennifer spread a slice of toast with the imported orange marmalade her mother loved.

"So, tell me about Troy," Patty said through a mouthful of eggs.

"I've been thinking. So much has been stolen from stores at the mall lately. Maybe it isn't because of shoplifting. After all, some of the equipment taken from SuperCharged would be awfully difficult to walk out the door with during business hours. You can't exactly stuff a CD changer or TV into your pocket."

"But a security guard like Troy could cart off just

about anything at night when no one's around?" Patty guessed.

"Right." Jennifer hesitated. "But it might be even worse than that. Suppose old Eleanor saw Troy, and he was afraid she'd rat on him."

Patty put down her fork and stared at her. "Jeez, Jen, you think he *killed* her? Then he might have tried to do the same thing to you . . . except—"

"Except someone or something interrupted him, and he couldn't finish the job." Jennifer started trembling at the sound of her own words. She clasped her hands together on the table top to make them stop shaking. "There are so many loose ends, though. Who stopped him? And why hasn't he tried again?"

"Maybe he's waiting for the right moment," Patty whispered. "Oh, Jen, you'd better not see him anymore. If he got violent with you like he did with Mike in the restaurant . . . Oh, jeez—remember, he carries a *gun!* You have to tell someone . . . your dad or the sheriff!"

"I will," Jennifer promised, "soon. First, though, I have to make absolutely sure I'm right about him. I need proof."

"If I were you, I wouldn't wait another day," Patty advised. She sighed and took a tiny bite of her eggs, looking as if she'd lost her appetite. "Just think, your boyfriend is a murderer . . ."

"He's *not* my boyfriend."

"Your lips may insist, but your heart tells me different," Patty insisted sadly.

"Don't say that!" Jennifer groaned. "I've spent all night trying to talk myself out of liking him. Come on, help me clean up. I have to get over to the mall before noon."

Patty came to life suddenly. "Wait—my dress! You brought it home with you the other night."

"I forgot all about it," Jennifer apologized. "Your tote bag's still in the trunk of my car."

The girls loaded dirty dishes into the dishwasher and returned milk, butter, and marmalade to the refrigerator. Then Jennifer ran out to her car and retrieved Patty's bag. Together they went upstairs to her bedroom.

It was an outrageously feminine room, and Jennifer loved it. Pink and white rosebud wallpaper, lace curtains enclosing an antique four-poster bed, and an elegant bleached-pine bureau. A dainty dressing table with a ruffled stool stood beneath an oval mirror circled by lights. Stuffed animals lined shelves built into all four walls. One day, she'd counted the plush toys: 234 in all. She'd collected them since she was a baby.

"Try on the dress so I can see you in it," Jennifer said.

"You really want me to?" Patty asked.

"Sure. You're wearing it to Homecoming, aren't you?"

"If I get up the nerve to ask Mike," Patty groaned. "A movie is one thing. But a formal dance means the guy has to rent a tuxedo, buy a corsage, and make dinner reservations. I don't know if Mike has the money to . . ."

Jennifer remembered Mike's expensive taste in clothes. "I'm sure he can scrape it up somewhere," she said dryly.

Patty pulled the sparkly red fabric out of the canvas bag and laid it carefully on the bed while she wiggled out of her jeans and T-shirt. Stepping into the dress, she pulled it up and slipped her arms through elastic straps.

"Zip me, please," she asked.

Jennifer accommodated her then stood back to admire the finished product. "You look positively steamy!" she announced. "That dress is worth every penny. How much did you say it cost? Two hundred something?"

"It doesn't matter," Patty said hastily, admiring herself in the full length mirror on Jennifer's closet as she smoothed her palms over her hips. "I love it, and Mike will love me in it."

Jennifer frowned at the intensity in her friend's eyes. Something wasn't quite right. "You must have had to bring back a ton of your other new stuff to afford this one dress," she said slowly.

"Uh, yeah," Patty mumbled. "But, like you said, it was worth it. Don't you think?"

Jennifer studied Patty, then the roomy tote. It was empty now. Patty must have brought it to work especially for the dress. She must have planned ahead to bring it out of Maxie's on her break.

A terrible feeling crept over Jennifer. Suddenly she doubted Patty's story about buying the red dress.

"Change back into your other clothes. I have to cut out of here soon," she said abruptly.

"I hate to take it off." Patty continued admiring herself in the mirror. "It makes me look so grown-up."

"Yeah. Well, as my grandma used to say, all good things must come to an end."

After Patty had left, Jennifer returned to her room. She dragged a brush through her long hair with vicious yanks, muttering with each stroke.

"Why didn't . . . you want . . . to put . . . your bag in . . . your own car, Patricia? Why did you . . . make me take it?"

The answer was, sadly, too easy. Patty had mentioned that the store where she worked had beefed up their security and were inspecting employees' bags. But if Patty had bought the dress, why was she so worried about security hassling her? All she had to do was show them her sales receipt . . . if she *had* a sales receipt!

But there was no way Patty could ever have afforded that dress. She never saved any money. Cash slipped through her fingers as easily as grains of sand.

Jennifer shook her head in disbelief. Not only had she

fallen for a boy who carried a gun, but her best friend was a thief. Who could she trust?

Troy reported for work at the mall, entering through the employees entrance. He punched in, picked up his walkie-talkie and keys, and checked the daily activity report.

Two of his fellow guards had observed a pair of twelve-year-old boys snatching purses and wallets in the food court. Working as a team, one distracted the victim by asking directions to a store, while the other deftly coaxed bills out of pockets and wallets from purses.

The guards had caught them with a bunch of stolen credit cards and five hundred in cash between them. A sheriff's deputy had taken the kids away. Troy hoped they'd learned a lesson, but knew throwing a scare into a kid didn't always work. Some grew up tough no matter what. Some like Mike Foley.

Troy spent the afternoon in his usual way, responding to calls from store managers when they spotted a likely shoplifter.

He saw Jennifer several times during the day but didn't stop to speak to her. She seemed to be a hard worker. She rolled out dough, shaped and baked the buns, and took several turns waiting on customers at the cash register. She did things carefully, he noticed, making the buns neat and round with just the right amount of caramel running over the top and down the sides. She was always polite to customers, asking them if they'd like extra napkins or something to drink with their order. She wished them a nice day and smiled pleasantly even if they didn't.

Jennifer was a really nice girl, and he liked her a lot. He wished he could get to know her better. But letting her come too close to him would almost certainly put her in danger, he reminded himself. He made a point of avoiding her.

When it began to get dark, Troy started looking around for Mike, who'd promised to meet him in front of the video arcade after he got off work. Troy spotted him on his seven o'clock rounds. Mike was wearing his usual black outfit, including shiny patent leather shoes and the long, full overcoat.

Troy came up behind him. "How's it going?" he asked in a low voice.

Mike nearly jumped out of his skin. "Man, don't do that!"

Troy hid a smile. "Didn't mean to scare you, buddy."

"I'm not your buddy. This is a business relationship. Remember?"

"Right," Troy said. "You ready to start working?"

Mike nodded, grinning as a couple of girls in short skirts passed by. Rocking back on his heels, he called out, " 'Lo, ladies, anything I can do for you?"

The girls ignored him and kept on walking.

"I don't think they like you, Mike." Troy took him loosely by the arm and started moving toward the exit. "Besides, why look any further? That girl at the restaurant seemed pretty crazy about you."

"Patty?" Mike sighed. "She's an old friend and a nice kid. Used to go with my brother."

"Really?"

"Yeah. She should find a guy like herself . . . smart and good-looking."

"Well, you're not dumb," Troy remarked as they stepped through the doors and onto the upper level parking pad.

Mike laughed. "But I ain't exactly pretty, is that it?"

"Well, of course, I'm no judge, being a guy myself. But I sort of suspect you might look better without that Darth Vader getup."

Mike huffed. "The clothes serve a purpose. You gotta intimidate sometimes to get to the truth."

"Well, it hasn't worked yet," Troy pointed out. "I think it's time to try something different."

Mike looked around. "Where are we going?" he asked as they continued down a row of cars.

The sun was hanging low in the wide, flat Texas sky. A typical Saturday after-dinner crowd was gathering as dusk thickened. Since the stores remained open until ten o'clock, folks would drift in to socialize while window shopping, or to kill time before a movie. But in the direction Troy and Mike were headed, the cars grew thinner, and the lights fewer.

"We're going to talk to a couple of people," Troy said.

"Out here in the lot?" Mike asked.

"Over there." Troy pointed to a beat-up station wagon with its tailgate open. A white sedan was slowly crossing the parking area. It stopped beside the wagon.

"Bart Boyleston and his wife? You won't get anything out of them. I already tried."

"Maybe not. But it's worth another shot."

Troy and Mike closed in on the man and woman who wore patched jeans, fringed suede jackets, and grimy Western hats. Mrs. Boyleston—everyone called her Butch when she wasn't around to hear—was taller than her squat, bearded husband. An ugly scar underlined her left eye. It was rumored a former boyfriend had given it to her when he discovered she'd been unfaithful to him.

Neither of them seemed to have a regular job. They apparently supported themselves by their profitable but illegal business buying beer and hard liquor in the nearest wet town and reselling it to kids in neighboring dry towns like McCarter.

As Troy and Mike approached, Bart spotted them. There was a flurry of activity and the sedan moved away with a squeal of tires.

Bart stepped forward to stall the intruders while his

wife hastily closed up the back end of the wagon. "What you want, Mr. Security?"

"Didn't I tell you to move out of here?" Troy demanded. "I'll call the sheriff again on you, Bart."

"Hey, we ain't doin' no harm." He slung an arm around his beloved. "Just me and the missus enjoyin' a moonlit night."

Butch gave her husband a sour look and stepped away. "We're perfectly within our rights to be here," she muttered.

"If I searched the back end of that car and found it loaded with booze, you'd have some explaining to do," Troy pointed out.

"You need a warrant," she snapped without hesitation.

"I could get one."

"We'd be gone by the time you came back with it," Bart countered. He jerked a thumb at Mike. "What's he doin' here?"

"He's out for some air. Listen, I want to ask you a few questions. Since you're law-abiding citizens, I'm sure you won't mind."

Bart and Butch exchanged wary glances.

"What kind of questions?" Bart asked.

"About Mike's brother Pete. He died about a year ago. Mike would like to know a little more about how it happened."

"How would we know?" Butch demanded impatiently, propping her rump against a rusting fender.

"You spend a lot of time hanging out hereabouts," Troy pointed out casually. "Maybe you saw something."

"Your friend already asked us," Bart said. "We didn't see nothin'."

"Maybe that was a long time ago, and you've remembered something since then," Troy suggested.

"Nothin'," Butch repeated, winding a strand of dirty hair around one finger.

Mike was circling the car, studying it as if he were a prospective buyer on a used car lot. Checking out the wiper blades, kicking the front right tire, flicking a scratch in the finish with one fingertip to test its depth.

"Hey, back off from the car!" Bart warned him.

Troy couldn't figure out what Mike was up to, but let him do his own thing. "Did you see Pete Foley anywhere around town on October twenty-ninth . . . the day he died? Think about it a minute. It was a hot day for this time of year. Got up to eighty-five. Kids were getting ready for Halloween parties. Your business must have been brisk," he added without humor.

Mike kicked the left front tire, hard.

"Hey, jerk!" Butch yelled. "He said, *back off!*"

"We didn't see the kid nowhere," Bart persisted, his eyes shifting worriedly to keep Mike in view.

What happened next probably didn't make Bart feel any better.

Mike nonchalantly stepped onto the bumper of the station wagon, walked up onto the hood, and began jumping up and down.

"Nice shocks!" he called down to Troy. "See, I can jump real hard, and she hardly bounces at all . . . built to carry a heavy load. Whoops! Look at that, I made a big dent! Guess this baby's not as tough as she looks."

"What the hell are you doing to my car?" Bart roared, running around to the front. "You're wreckin' my car, you bozo!"

"Wrecking your car?" Mike looked offended. He thrust his hands into his coat pockets and stood erect on the hood, his tall, dark figure silhouetted in the parking lot lamps. "If I were wrecking your car, you'd know it. I'd be doing something like *this!*" He lifted one foot and smashed the heavy shoe heel into the windshield, leaving a hairline crack. "Or *this!*" His second strike sent spider web lines shooting across the safety glass.

Troy stepped forward to stop Mike, then thought better about interrupting him. He'd bet a month's pay that Bart had stolen the wagon. Considering the mess it was already, he was sure the owners would prefer the insurance money to getting their car back. Besides, if Mike got the Boylestons riled up enough, maybe they'd let something slip.

"Stop him!" Butch demanded, glaring furiously at Troy. "He's destroying personal property. You're supposed to be the law around here, aren't you?"

Troy sighed dramatically. "Technically, my jurisdiction ends once I leave the mall building. Of course, I could walk back and call the sheriff to report the vandalism of your car. A dispatcher would send a car over, but I suspect Mike wouldn't wait around for him."

"What do you *want?*" Bart yelled. "You're either crazy or you want something! So what is it?"

Mike stopped kicking the windshield and stepped back to admire his work. With a satisfied nod, he turned around, sat on the roof of the car, leaned forward and took hold of one of the windshield wiper blades in both hands. With the concentration of an artist creating his masterpiece, he twisted the blade into a fine-looking corkscrew design.

"He's freakin' lost his mind!" Bart screamed while his wife reached up to swipe at Mike with her fist. He merely moved out of range to the opposite side of the windshield and began bending the other blade.

"Actually, I think the poor kid's frustrated," Troy remarked philosophically. "You know how it is—idle hands are the devil's tools. He really wants to find out what happened to his brother. Until he does, he needs these emotional outlets . . ."

"I *saw* the kid!" gasped Bart.

Butch turned on him with a look of horror in her dull eyes. "Shut up, you moron!"

"He's wreckin' my car! What do you want me to do? Stand here and let him!" Bart wiped the sweat from his hairy upper lip. "I saw him . . . Pete Foley. I know it was him and I know it was that night because the next day his picture was in all the papers . . . hanging from the goalpost like a Halloween scarecrow and all." He lowered his voice so Mike wouldn't hear. "We had a chuckle over it, me and the old lady. He looked kinda funny, know what I mean?"

Troy didn't let his disgust show. "Where was Pete when you saw him?" he asked coldly.

Mike took out his keys and started scratching his initials in an uncracked portion of windshield. With a shriek, Butch flung open one of the rear doors and ducked inside to rummage through a pile of junk.

"He was walking down San Jacinto between here and the movie theater," Bart said.

"Which way?"

"This way, like he was going to the mall."

"Was anyone with him?"

"No."

"What time was it?"

"Eleven. No—later. Eleven-thirty or so."

"Did you see him again that night?"

Bart hesitated for a brief instant. He glanced toward the open car door where his wife's legs stuck out. "No," he repeated. "That was the last time I saw him."

Butch emerged with a baseball bat in hand and a look of unreliable fury on her face. "Get down offa that car *now*, creep!" she snarled, brandishing the bat.

Mike peered down at her, then turned to Troy. "Are we all done?" he asked calmly. "Cause I'm getting pretty bored sitting around waiting while you guys chat."

"We're done for now," Troy said, covering his smile with one hand. "Let's go."

Troy had never laughed so hard as in the first ten minutes after he and Mike left the Boylestons in the mall parking lot, assessing the damage done to their car.

"Under any other circumstances," Troy gasped, holding his sides, "I couldn't have let you do that."

Mike shook his head, unable to speak he was laughing so hard. At last he made a brave attempt. "Y-y-you . . . you . . . you should have seen the looks on their faces when I kicked the windshield the . . . the f-f-first time. They figured I'd completely lost my marbles."

"They're probably right."

Mike dissolved into chuckles again. "Man, it feels so good to laugh. I don't think I've laughed once since Pete died." His grin softened into a reminiscent smile. "Pete loved to laugh. He made other people happy too. He was a good guy . . . better than me."

"That remains to be seen," Troy said quietly. "You have a lot of time to do good things in your life."

Mike looked at him, suddenly serious again. "Thanks, man. Thanks a lot."

"For what?"

"For trusting me. Believing in me." He paused and glanced down at his hands, "So, what are you going to do to me, Mr. Security Guard? I did bust up their car. I'll pay for damages."

"I don't think that'll be necessary. The Boylestons had trashed that car before you got to it."

Mike nodded, looking relieved. "So, what did Bart tell you? I was making so much noise I couldn't hear."

"He admitted seeing Pete the night he died."

Mike twisted around to stare across the lot at the couple. "No joke."

"No. And I think he was telling the truth. He was so

distracted by your act, he'd stopped thinking defensively."

"Where was Pete?"

"Walking between the theater and the mall, at about eleven-thirty that night."

Mike winced as if someone had punched him hard in the gut. "He'd taken Patty to a show and walked her home. I had my parents' car. We'd argued about who should have it, and my dad said if we kept it up neither of us could take it. Pete backed off and let me have the wheels for the night."

"Why was he walking to the mall at that hour?" Troy asked. "It was closed."

"I don't know." Mike considered the question. "Maybe he wasn't. Maybe he was just walking, you know, because it was hot out, or he'd had a fight with Patty, or . . ." He dropped his head. "Man, I don't know."

Troy weighed his options. He ought to go back inside. It was getting near closing time. He had to padlock the four loading dock gates, secure the employee entrance, and make sure all the customers were out before the main doors were locked for the night. The elevator was still acting up too.

Make sure everyone is out, he mused.

"What is it? You just figured something out, didn't you?" Mike asked excitedly. "I saw that look on your face."

"It's just an idea . . . something we have to follow up on." Then another thought occurred to Troy, which made his blood run as cold as an Alaskan night. "Jennifer's in danger."

"Huh?"

"Jennifer . . . the girl who was attacked at the mall a few weeks ago."

"Was she the one at the restaurant with you? Patty's friend?"

"Yeah." Troy instantly saw her in his mind. Her dark hair had glistened like silk in the restaurant's lights. Her violet eyes were so full of life and curiosity . . . especially about him. He'd give anything to be able to tell her the truth. But that was impossible for the time being. "That was her. Someone almost killed her. And I have a feeling whoever it is will try again. Probably soon."

"Why?"

"Because she's the only one who survived." He looked hard at Mike. The boy didn't get it. "Three people died, or *almost* died violent deaths in East McCarter, a town that has almost no crime," Troy explained. "Pete was on his way to the mall. Eleanor Duvall and her friends hung out in the mall tunnels at night. And Jennifer was trying to take a shortcut out of the building to her car. Only she's still alive. There must be some reason why."

"So, what's the next step?"

"You and I have to track down old Eleanor's friends and talk with them."

"Man!" Mike laughed. "They won't talk to no one."

"I know, and if they don't want to be found in the mall, they'll disappear down a maze of alleys and utility tunnels. But together we might have a shot of taking them by surprise. I'm hoping they saw whatever Eleanor saw."

"Like they'll tell you, sure." Mike shook his head. "Why not ask 'em to sign their own death certificates?"

"If I can convince them that they'll be safe, they might be willing to talk to me."

Mike looked doubtful. "No harm in trying, I guess. But what about Jennifer? I mean, if someone's out to get her . . ."

"You're right," Troy admitted. "I'll have to stick close to her to protect her."

Mike dropped an arm around Troy's shoulder and grinned at him. "Nice work if you can get it."

* * *

After leaving Troy at the mall, Mike cut across the football field behind McCarter High, taking the same route between his house and the mall that he took every evening because it was half as long as any other. On his way he passed the goalposts where his brother's body had been found.

It used to be that he couldn't walk past this spot without weeping. Pete had been such a good kid.

"It should have been me," Mike whispered for the hundredth time as he walked faster, anxious to get away from the place.

When it happened, almost a year ago, he'd gone crazy with rage at the world. He'd dropped out of high school and cut himself from off from his friends. All that mattered was getting even. *I'll get them. I'll massacre whoever did this to you, Pete! If it kills me, I'll get them.*

Gradually his fury took shape in a plan. He found a job in a meat-packing plant in Houston, where nobody knew him. Every day, he rode the bus into the city and back home, because he didn't want to spend money on a car and refused to drive his mother's . . . the one he and Pete had sometimes shared and had argued about *that night.*

He needed every cent he could get his hands on to buy expensive clothes and the few samples of crack and cocaine he carried on him. He made several buys from a local pusher to further his reputation as a small-time dealer. But as soon as he got home he always flushed the junk down the toilet.

The clothes, the dope, the way he walked and talked . . . everything was intended to help him mix with the slime of society, for he figured only slime would have killed someone as perfect as Pete. And somewhere, some low-life creep had to know the truth about how his brother had died, because guys who wasted other guys were stupid. They talked about it.

A couple of years ago, a Texas Ranger had been shot and killed when he'd stopped a car on the highway. No one had a clue who'd done it . . . until the ranger's murderer got drunk one night in a Dallas bar and boasted about how he'd put the gun to the ranger's head and pulled the trigger. One of his scummy friends turned him in for the reward money.

Sooner or later he'd hear a name . . . stumble on a reason. Then he'd hunt the bastard down, with or without Troy's help.

Chapter 10

JENNIFER LOOKED UP from the dough mixer at the flour caking her fingers. With the back of one hand, she brushed a stray hair out of her eyes, leaving a trail of white powder across her cheekbone. For the sixth or seventh time that evening, she had the distinct feeling that someone was watching her. And, for the sixth or seventh time, she peered into the crowd passing Caramelbun and spotted Troy lingering in front of the shoe store across the way.

She couldn't decide if she was flattered or frightened by his interest in her. To follow him around was one thing. But to *be* followed made her feel as if she were being stalked, and she much preferred the role of hunter to that of the hunted.

Her father telephoned from SuperCharged at eight o'clock. "Are you still planning on leaving at ninethirty?" he asked.

Since she'd returned to work he often called to make sure of her hours and ask what time she expected be home. She tried to reassure him that she'd be safe—although she couldn't talk herself out of the fear that always returned with darkness.

Thinking about the night that had almost been her last, she touched the wicked scar around her throat. As the healing progressed, the scabs often itched, as if to remind her: *The terror is real! It could happen again!*

"I'll be fine, Daddy." She wanted to reassure him

and hoped her voice sounded confident. "I should be home before ten."

However, at nine o'clock, Jerry received a phone call from his wife. After a few words, he hung up and walked over to Jennifer. "How's it going tonight?"

"Okay," she replied.

"Want a break?"

"Naw." She lifted the heavy stainless steel bowl and dumped out a mountain of white dough on the marble slab. "I leave in half an hour."

Jerry grimaced. "I wanted to talk to you about that. I haven't asked you to close since the night you got hurt. But my wife just called to say Angie is sick." Angie was his baby daughter. She was a little over five months old. "Tracy's pretty new. I don't think I can leave her to close alone."

Jennifer swallowed hard and tried not to show her nervousness. "Go ahead on home. We'll be fine."

"You're sure?" Jerry asked guiltily. "I mean, at least you won't be alone."

"No problem. I'll ask one of the security guards to walk me to my car."

"Thanks, Jennifer." He smiled at her. "By the way, I wanted to tell you—it took a lot of guts to come back the way you did. You're a lot tougher than you look."

She wished she *looked* a lot tougher. Then whoever had come after her might not be tempted to try it again.

Jennifer worked quickly, showing Tracy the closing procedures—wiping down the counters with a diluted bleach solution, sweeping then wet-mopping the floor, storing ingredients in the walk-in refrigerator in the back, counting up the day's cash, checks, and charge card receipts, then entering code numbers into the register to lock it for the night.

A few other employees were locking up their stores. They wandered off in various directions.

"I'll drop off the cash bag at the bank on my way

out," she told the other girl. "Next time, you can do it."

"Thanks for your help, Jennifer," Tracy said pleasantly. "My dad's here to pick me up. Okay if I leave?"

"Sure."

Then, despite Jerry's promise, she was alone.

The memory of *that* night closed around her like fingers of a dreadful hand, choking off her breath.

Trembling, Jennifer looped her purse over one shoulder and tucked the canvas deposit bag under one arm. She started off at a frantic jog toward the bank.

As she rounded the corner, she almost crashed into someone headed the other way. It was Troy.

"Hi!" he said almost too cheerfully for their meeting to be coincidence. "Where are you off to?"

Jennifer swallowed, studying him, trying to quiet her racing heart. "McCarter Federal." She held up the bag. "Then home."

"Want some company?"

For some reason, she found herself nodding yes as lights in the corridor dimmed. She definitely welcomed his protection from whatever might be lurking in a deserted tunnel or outside on the parking lot. But her eyes fixed on the slight bulge beneath his shirt, knowing the gun was there, and she felt the chill of fear that always seemed to hang over their meetings. If Troy was indeed involved in the things that had been happening at the mall, he was the last person in the world to trust or expect help from. So why did she want so badly to trust him? Why couldn't she stay away from him?

Jennifer made a point of waving and loudly calling out good-byes to the few people they passed. If someone pulled her body out of a trash bin in the morning, a half dozen witnesses would come forward to attest to the fact she'd last been seen with Troy. Not that postmortem revenge was much consolation, but it was better than nothing.

"I saw you around a lot tonight," she commented as she dropped the cash pouch into the metal deposit slot.

"Yeah? I was pretty busy tonight . . . running all over the place."

She couldn't resist teasing him. "You mean, in between shopping for shoes?"

His face flushed, and he looked flustered.

"I saw you studying shoes at Bargain Buys. You seemed very interested in them."

"There were a couple nice pairs . . . for the money," Troy commented defensively. Then he gave up and grinned at her. "Pretty obvious, huh?"

"Yeah." A warm tingle radiated through her bones, although she knew she shouldn't let down her defenses.

"Is your car in the usual place? Second level?"

She nodded, and when he reached for her hand she couldn't resist slipping her fingers into his warm grip. Automatically, her free hand reached up to touch the scar at her throat. *No,* she told herself firmly, trying to make herself believe, *not Troy. He wouldn't hurt me.*

Jennifer chattered away about the day, about what it was like being a senior at McCarter High, and about her upcoming tennis matches . . . anything to chase away the dark doubts.

"I can't expect to win my next match," she told him. "My opponent is very good, and I've been working on a new backhand. Whenever you change your technique, even a little, it affects your whole game and takes a while for you to come back to full power."

"I'd like to see you play sometime," he said.

Pleased, but still wary, Jennifer gave him a small smile. "My next match is Thursday. But I'd rather you wait another week to come and watch. I'll be in better form by then."

"Okay," he agreed.

They must have been walking slower than everyone else. By the time they reached the area near the fountain no one was in sight. The stone benches were empty, the elevator that only moved up and down one floor was motionless, even the speakers that usually provided cheery shopping music were ominously silent.

As they walked toward the stairs leading up to the second level, Troy cast an irritated look at the elevator. The call button remained lit, although they'd seen no one around who might have pushed it.

"Stupid thing must be acting up again. I'll have to call the elevator company if I can't fix it myself. Mall Management will be PO'd for sure. They hate paying for expensive service calls."

Looking back over her shoulder, Jennifer spotted something odd. "Look!" She pointed to a brightly colored object wedged beneath the closed doors.

"Hold on a minute," Troy said.

Jennifer stood by while he repeatedly punched the call button with his thumb to make the doors open. Nothing happened.

Troy wedged his fingers between the two doors and tried to pull them apart.

"Maybe you should leave it for the repairmen," she suggested. "Machinery that big and heavy could be dangerous."

Stepping back, Troy raked a hand through his hair. "When I see something broken, I just can't leave it alone. It's like a puzzle."

He stooped and tugged on the object stuck beneath the door, his gray eyes sparkling with curiosity. But his fingers kept slipping off the smooth plastic.

"I should be able to force the doors . . ." he muttered, looking around as if for something to jam between the metal sliders. When he couldn't find anything, he tried again with his hands.

Jennifer stepped closer. "Troy, please leave it alone. What if—"

"You worry too much."

Jennifer sighed. She'd learned, after a couple boyfriends, that arguing with a guy over anything mechanical was a waste of time.

"I can help," she offered at last, pushing her fingers between the two door halves lower down. Together they grunted, and shoved, and, slowly, the doors ground open.

"Hey, don't!" a shout echoed through the empty corridor. It was Gary. "Jennifer, stay away from there!"

If she released her hold, the doors would slam closed on Troy. "I'm fine," she grunted. "Troy needs help with the elevator. Something's caught in it."

Gary ran up to them, a TV remote control still in one hand. "Get away!" he pleaded, his voice taut, rising in pitch. "You could get hurt!"

Jennifer ignored him.

"I think I've . . . got it." Reaching out with his right foot, Troy kicked a red plastic windshield scraper from between the doors.

Jennifer looked inside the shaft to see a maze of cables and pulleys, and the oily motor that must have driven the elevator. "The car is on the second level," she commented, straining against the doors. Then she saw something else . . . something that made her blood freeze in her veins. "Look! Look at that!"

"What?" Troy squinted, then at last saw it too. "A garrote!" he choked out.

"What?" Jennifer asked.

"A rope with a knot in the middle. If you want to strangle someone you don't just use a plain rope, it takes too much strength. A knot in the middle breaks the windpipe," Troy explained grimly.

Jennifer squeezed her eyes shut in horror. Was this what had been used on her?

"Can you hold on a little longer?" Troy asked. "I have to try to get that thing out of the shaft."

"I think so," she murmured shakily.

"Oh, God!" Gary wailed. "Someone's gonna get killed. Leave it alone!"

Troy seemed to realize for the first time that Gary was there. "Come here, man. Give Jennifer a hand."

The boy took a step backward, an expression of horror crossing his face. "Are you crazy? We could get crushed!"

Jennifer's fingers cramped painfully, and she let out a soft whimper.

"Grab the door!" Troy ordered. "She's not strong enough to hold it any longer!"

With a muffled curse, Gary stepped forward and wrapped his fingers around the edge of the door. Jennifer released her hold and staggered out of the way, flexing the blood back into her numb fingers.

She stood back, watching nervously as Troy pressed his body into the gap between the doors.

"Don't let go!" he shouted at Gary, then jumped off of the first floor into the shallow pit. Only his head and shoulders showed above the floor.

"Hurry!" Gary cried. "The doors . . . I can't hold them . . . much longer!"

"Just one more minute!" Troy shouted. His voice was muffled as he bent over, one hand still taking some of the weight of the elevator door.

At that moment, Gary twisted around and stared at the TV controller he'd shoved into his back pocket. Leaning one shoulder against the edge of the door to keep it from closing, he reached for the black plastic pad.

Dad will kill him if that gets smashed, Jennifer thought, which was undoubtedly Gary's fear.

"I'll hold it," she offered.

But as she stretched out one hand to take the control from him, a whirring noise caught her attention and she sensed sudden movement from above.

"Troy! Look out!" Jennifer screamed.

Everything seemed to happen in slow motion, yet quicker than her brain could absorb. The elevator compartment descended on Troy at the same moment that he looked up at it with a shocked expression.

Releasing a terrified shriek, Gary let go of the door and jumped back.

"Get out! Get out!" Jennifer screamed, rushing forward. But Troy couldn't hold the door open and climb out at the same time.

Without thinking about the danger she was putting herself in, Jennifer braced her back against one door and pressed both her hands against the opposite side. She pushed with all her strength. The tendons in her arms and legs knotted, feeling as if they were tearing.

With the garrote clutched in one hand, Troy exploded up out of the shaft a split second ahead of the speeding elevator compartment. Jennifer collapsed on the floor, gasping for air and wiping away tears of relief as the doors slammed shut.

"Brother, was that close!" she cried.

Then she saw the blood.

Jennifer's mouth dropped open as she watched a vicious red stain seep through the shredded pant leg of Troy's uniform. Blood trickled down his ankle and shoe, rapidly forming a pool on the floor. As Troy leaned against the glass elevator casing, he rested his forehead on one arm and closed his eyes against the pain.

"Oh, man!" Gary exclaimed. "You're hurt bad." He started running toward SuperCharged while shouting back at Jennifer, "I'll call for help."

Chapter 11

"I DON'T KNOW HOW it happened," Jennifer repeated for the third time, tears rolling down her cheeks. "Troy was walking me to my car. He noticed that something was wrong with the elevator. He tried to fix it, but it . . . it . . . it," she hiccupped helplessly, "it came crashing down on him!"

Her stomach spasmed, and a taste of sour bile rose into her throat and mouth. *I won't puke!* she told herself, holding her head in trembling hands. *I won't! I won't. I won't!*

The sheriff had arrived at the hospital moments after ambulance attendants wheeled Troy into the Emergency Room. *The sheriff's office must monitor accident calls,* she'd thought vaguely. As far as she knew, Gary had only called for medical assistance.

Now, after waiting for over an hour in the hospital lounge without any word of Troy's condition, she was crazy with fear. And the sheriff wasn't helping with his constant questions.

"Please!" she cried. "I don't know anything. Can I see Troy now?"

"When the doctor says it's okay," the sheriff repeated gruffly. "Did you see anyone around the elevator as you and Troy approached it?"

"No. I told you before. We were the only ones in that part of the mall."

"No one at all?" he persisted.

She shook her head. "Gary Pyzik came out of SuperCharged when he saw Troy messing around with the elevator. He tried to warn us away. He was the only one."

The sheriff scratched the shadow of beard on his chin and snapped closed his pocket notepad. He was sitting beside Jennifer on a plastic upholstered couch in the waiting room. Looking hard at Jennifer, he said in a solemn voice, "Troy told me that you saved his life."

She was surprised. "I . . . I suppose I did. I didn't really think about it at the time."

"Sheriff?" a voice called from the waiting room door.

They both looked up to see a middle-aged man in a sport shirt and cords. Jennifer suspected he was the doctor who'd been called in to treat Troy. The two men spoke in subdued voices, too low for her to hear. Then, as if they were about to leave, they suddenly turned toward the doorway leading to the treatment rooms.

"Hey! What about me?" Jennifer demanded, pushing herself onto her feet. She felt wobbly from exhaustion. The muscles in her arms and legs throbbed. "May I *please* see Troy?"

The doctor looked at the sheriff.

"After I have a word with him," the lawman said. "Wait here."

Jennifer paced the waiting area for what felt like an eternity. Two young men shared the floor space with her. She supposed they were expectant fathers, but she didn't ask. Nothing mattered except Troy at this moment.

She couldn't understand why the doctor was stalling her. Maybe Troy was in worse shape than she thought and the authorities needed to take his statement before he . . .

She squeezed her eyes shut, unable to even think the word.

Finally, a nurse peeked around the corner. "Are you Jennifer?"

"Yes!" she shouted, almost running over the woman in her rush to see Troy. "Where?"

"Third door on the left."

Jennifer tore down a mint green hallway that smelled strongly of disinfectant, plaster powder, and the warm, sickeningly sweet scent of blood. *No matter how bad he is . . . how repulsive he looks . . . I will not let him know!*

To her surprise, Troy was standing up and gazing out a window that overlooked the hospital parking lot. His uniform slacks must have been ruined. He wore what appeared to be a surgeon's baggy cotton pants. Their loose fit allowed for the thick bandages she could see filling out Troy's left thigh.

"Hi, Jen," he said softly without turning to face her.

She smiled timidly. "I figured you'd be stretched out on a bed, unconscious or something."

"A lot of blood, some bad scrapes, not much more." He turned around and gave her an encouraging grin. "I don't think I'll be sitting down for a while though." He gently patted his rear end.

She laughed, walked over to him, and kissed him lightly on the cheek. "I'm glad you're all right. I was scared."

"When I saw that elevator coming at me, I was too," he admitted. "Thanks." Then his expression deepened. "I have to tell you something. Sit down, Jen."

Perching obediently on the edge of the windowsill, she looked up at him. He stepped over in front of her and took her hands.

"I had to get permission from the sheriff to tell you this," he began. "Believe me, it wasn't easy. He doesn't think it's a good idea, but I insisted that you could be trusted. You can't repeat what I'm going to tell you to anyone. Not to Patty, your friends on the tennis team, or even your parents. Not to *anyone!* Understand?"

She nodded, intrigued by his mysterious tone.

"I'm not who you think I am," he whispered.

Her heart missed two beats before she realized he couldn't be telling her that he was a thief and murderer. After all, why would he ask a lawman's permission to tell her that?

"I'm a student at the University of Texas in Austin," he continued.

She laughed. "If you want to impress me, try a more believable line. I haven't noticed you making time in your schedule for classes. Anyway, the university is too far away to commute to from McCarter."

"I'm serious, Jen. I'm taking a prelaw course specializing in the criminal justice system. Someday I hope to join the FBI."

"So, what does that have to do with being a security guard at McCarter Mall?" she asked skeptically.

"I had the opportunity to sign up for a student internship with a state law enforcement agency. Most of the time students are assigned clerical duties, or ride along with deputies from one of the local sheriff's offices and take notes. Nothing very exciting, but it's good experience. Sheriff Patterson needed someone to work undercover, someone young who could pose as a part-time guard and maybe mix with the local kids. He asked me if I'd do it. I said yes."

Jennifer stared at Troy, trying to understand what he was telling her. "You're a cop?"

"Sort of . . . temporarily . . ."

"Then, what about *us?*" she asked. "I mean . . . I guess there isn't an *us*. Is there?"

Troy shook his head sadly. "I really liked you . . . I still do. But I'm not in McCarter to shop for a girlfriend."

"I see," she said slowly, her heart shriveling up in her chest like a desert blossom.

"It's just the wrong time, Jen. I'm sorry. If I think about you, I can't concentrate on my job."

"And exactly what is your job . . . your undercover work?"

"You can't tell anyone."

"I won't," she promised, "not a soul."

He drew a deep breath. "The sheriff suspects that Pete Foley's suicide was rigged. Certain evidence . . . the way the rope was knotted around his throat . . . strange bruises on areas of his neck and head that couldn't have been caused by the rope . . . they all point to someone else being at the scene, and to Pete putting up a struggle."

"Poor Pete," Jennifer whispered.

"But there were no fingerprints anywhere, no footprints on the hard ground, nothing to point to his executioner. Not until Eleanor Duvall was murdered at the mall six months later."

"I don't understand . . . what could Pete Foley and a homeless old lady have in common?"

"That's what Sheriff Patterson wanted to know . . . because the bruises around their throats seemed too similar to be coincidental."

Jennifer walked over to a mirror on the other side of the room. She pulled the turtleneck jersey away from her neck and stared at the raw marks that scarred her throat. Two fading purple bruises still marked opposite sides of her neck.

"Like this?" she asked tightly.

Troy stepped over and gently touched one spot with two fingers. "Yes, like that. It's as if whoever attacked you came up from behind with a piece of thin rope or twine, looped it around your throat, pulled, then increased the pressure by wedging their thumbs against the sides of your neck." He pointed. "Here and here."

Closing her eyes, Jennifer shuddered. And suddenly, it was as if she were back in the dark tunnel, her breath ruthlessly cut off from her lungs, the world turning black . . . and she heard a voice calling her name.

Her eyes burst open, and she turned to stare at Troy. "It was someone who knows me!" she cried.

"What?"

"I remember . . . just before I lost consciousness. Someone cried out, 'Jennifer! Oh, no—Jennifer!'"

"Are you sure? Maybe it was me . . . when I saw you."

"No, I definitely heard the voice *before* I passed out," she insisted.

"You don't recognize who it was?"

"No," she said dismally. "The words were foggy sounding, distant . . . and my eyes must have been closed by then. So I couldn't have seen the person." She thought for a moment. "You still don't know who telephoned for the ambulance?"

"No. We've replayed the tape recorded by the 911 operator a hundred times. The voice is high and squeaky. Either a woman or a man pretending to be a woman. All the caller says is that a girl is badly hurt at the mall and needs medical attention . . . and that she's near the number four loading dock."

Jennifer nodded. Things were beginning to fit.

Troy concentrated on a spot on the floor, thinking out loud. "As soon as your attacker recognized you, he or she released the pressure on your throat, then anonymously summoned help."

"Or he was interrupted by someone else and ran off. Then that other person, the person whose voice I heard, made the call," Jennifer suggested.

Troy raked a hand through his short blond hair. "Yes . . . it could have happened that way too." He stared at her. "And the second scenario is worse, because it means that our murderer might still intend to finish the job."

Jennifer couldn't speak for several minutes she was so stunned by the results of her and Troy's speculations. It meant that Troy was no longer a suspect. She felt tremendously grateful that he was, after all, one of the good guys. On the other hand, she was no closer to learning who had tried to kill her.

"Can you give me a lift home?" Troy asked, interrupting her troubled thoughts.

"Sure," she said, glad that she wouldn't have to leave the hospital alone in the dark.

Troy sat lopsided in the passenger seat of the Miata, keeping as much as possible off of his injured thigh. He wanted more than anything to kiss Jennifer good night, but settled for thanking her again once they'd reached the motel.

"When I run into you at the mall, I'll let you know how the investigation is going," he promised. "Meanwhile, say nothing to anyone about this, and don't go anywhere alone. Stay in public places as much as possible."

"All right," she agreed.

He hated the way her smile no longer sparkled as brightly as when they'd first met. She was beautiful—her black hair gleaming under the street light, her violet eyes moist with disappointment. He didn't know what to say to her. *Jen, if you only knew how much I want to touch you.*

"Good night," he said stiffly, edging carefully off of the car seat.

She didn't answer. When she drove off, he was sure she was crying. He felt like crap.

It took him almost half an hour to fight his way out of the clothes he'd borrowed from Dr. Holliman and get comfortable in bed. He had to sleep on his stomach to stay off the wound on the back of his left leg where the elevator car had gouged out a healthy chunk. The surgeon had closed up the flesh pretty well, but it had taken almost a hundred tiny stitches to do the job.

Troy couldn't sleep for a long time. He thought about

Jennifer, Pete Foley, and Eleanor Duvall. They had several things in common.

They had all been at the mall late at night and had all seen something that someone wanted to deep secret badly enough to kill for. No, he corrected himself, they hadn't yet placed Pete at the mall. He was only seen walking in that direction.

Then something else occurred to him. If he could establish that Pete had actually been at the mall the night he died, it might be proven that he was actually killed *there*, then moved to the football field for a staged suicide.

Then what? Troy squeezed his eyes shut, trying to ignore his sore thigh. Who was pulling the strings behind the mall murders? Who?

Chapter 12

THE NEXT MORNING, Troy dug out a pair of old sweatpants loose enough to wear over his bandages. He felt stiff and sore but not bad considering he'd had a close brush with a two-ton elevator. Sitting on the edge of the motel bed, Troy dialed Mike Foley's home.

"Mike's at work," his mother explained.

"Do you have a number where I can reach him?" Troy asked.

"Sure. Hold on."

As soon as Troy had jotted down the Houston phone number, he thanked Mrs. Foley and redialed. A gruff male voice came on the line and said he'd get Mike. Several minutes passed. Troy impatiently tapped the scratched top of the bedside table.

Nothing he'd learned so far eliminated Mike from suspicion. But Troy had a feeling about the kid. His love for his brother rang true. And, as schizo as Mike sometimes behaved, Troy was beginning to believe that he was basically harmless . . . except maybe around cars.

At last, Mike picked up.

"Meet me at the mall at eight," Troy said.

Mike must have heard the tension in his voice. "What's wrong?"

"Something happened last night. We'll talk about it later."

"Right."

Troy wasn't scheduled to work that day, but he didn't

dare stay away from the mall for long, fearing something might happen to Jennifer. The shopping center was about two miles down the road. He intended to leave his truck in the mall lot until he could drive it more comfortably. If he had to go very far, he'd ask Mike to drive. Meanwhile, the exercise would be good for his injured leg.

On his way he'd pass the sheriff's office. Troy dropped in for an update.

"One of my men is pretty good with electronic gadgets," Sheriff Patterson told Troy. "He and a repairman from the elevator company went over the motor, wires, and all. They're fairly sure that somebody sabotaged the elevator by disabling the electric eye and triggering the car to descend at the moment you were in the shaft."

Troy scowled. "Sounds pretty sophisticated to me."

"It was a slick job, all right," the sheriff admitted. "They still can't figure out how anyone could do it without you seeing them. I suppose whoever it was must have been hiding on the upper level, then reached into the compartment and pushed the down button."

"Maybe there was some sort of timer," Troy suggested.

"Well," Patterson said, "they haven't found one yet. Besides, how would the guy know exactly when you'd be inside the shaft . . . or, for that matter, that you'd come anywhere near the elevator last night?"

Troy shook his head. "I don't know. But I suppose that once we figure out how it was done, we'll know who our killer is."

Sheriff Patterson looked at him solemnly. "Like I told you last night at the hospital, son . . . maybe now's the time you should back out of this project. I never intended for you to do more than keep your eyes open . . . pick up a few leads for us."

"I understand that." Troy looked away, thinking. "But I can't stop now. Please let me keep working with you. I feel as if I'm getting so close. If I weren't, the killer wouldn't have gone to the bother of rigging that elevator."

"True," admitted the sheriff. He looked hard at Troy, his kind eyes circled with deep worry lines. "Just you be careful, son. And if anything happens . . . anything at all, give a call. I've got men close by, round the clock."

Troy spent the afternoon investigating the maze of tunnels and passageways restricted from public use that linked the stores, loading docks, storage areas, and central power plant of the mall. As well as he knew his way around, he was surprised by the number of hidden away niches and remote alleys he'd never come across before. But he failed to discover anything out of the ordinary in any of them.

It was late afternoon before he began one of his last searches, the area behind the bookstore. Louise looked up from behind the cashier's counter as he passed.

"Not wearing your uniform today?" she commented.

"Had to wash it," Troy called out without stopping.

He moved quickly between the aisles of hardcover and paperback volumes then through the rear door marked Personnel Only. Boxes of books waiting to be unpacked and shelved almost completely filled the tight space. Turning sideways to squeeze between the stacks, Troy moved toward the back until he came upon a mountain of empty cartons. The light bulb in the socket overhead had burnt out, and there was only a black wall behind the boxes.

"Dead end," he muttered, disappointed.

But since he'd come this far and was running out of possibilities, he decided there was no harm in being thorough. Moving two cartons aside, he reached back as far as he could and his hand hit . . .

Nothing . . . only empty space.

Bingo! he thought exultantly. Anyone casually entering the storage area would never have guessed that the tunnel continued. Even the Books N Things clerks who realized there was something beyond this little room probably thought nothing of it.

Pulling down boxes, he rapidly created a space he could fit through. Then Troy drew a flashlight from his back pocket. He cautiously moved into the passage. It was free of cobwebs, as if somebody frequently came this way. After a hundred feet of bare cement walls and floor, Troy had just about decided he'd stumbled on yet another dead end, when the tunnel branched into two storage rooms. The one on the right was empty. The other answered his prayers.

The room was furnished with a lamp, which sat on a small square oak table, two lightweight upholstered chairs, and a folding table covered with a clean white vinyl tablecloth. Sitting atop two inflated mattresses was a neatly folded stack of blankets and pillows. A pair of packing crates turned on their sides served as a simple cupboard for plastic plates, cups, and eating utensils.

Slowly, Troy circled the room, studying everything . . . touching nothing. If the plan evolving in his mind worked properly, Patterson would have a fingerprint expert from Houston in here before the end of the week. However, there were other things he had to accomplish first.

Troy left everything as he'd found it and retraced his tracks into the public part of the mall.

At eight o'clock, as planned, he met Mike outside the video arcade. He was surprised to find the boy wearing ordinary jeans and a dark blue T-shirt instead of his usual sinister black costume.

"I went crazy waiting to get off work. You said on the phone that something happened. What?" he asked.

Troy told him about the elevator incident, while Mike listened in silence, his face growing rigid as he absorbed each detail.

"Man, you could have been squashed to death!"

"I know."

"Well, watch your back from now on! Someone means business!"

"I intend to." Troy studied Mike for a minute, wondering again if he was wise to trust him. Time would tell. But time was getting short. He started walking. "Come on, we have work to do."

"You said we'd track down those two winos," Mike reminded him.

"I doubt they're winos . . . more likely just two people without jobs or homes. But I'll be surprised if they don't know something about what's been going on in McCarter. I found their hideout."

"No kidding!" Mike looked excited.

"It's in a tunnel behind the bookstore, and there's only one way in or out. If they show up tonight, we'll have them cornered."

"Do you think they killed Pete and old Eleanor?"

"And tried to kill Jennifer? I don't think so," Troy said carefully.

"Why?"

"Evidence is beginning to point pretty strongly to someone else."

"Who?"

"I'd rather not say yet. I want to talk to these two first. If they've seen what I suspect, and will talk about it, we may find your brother's killer tonight."

Mike's fists clenched at his sides, and his eyes hardened to brittle black chips.

Reaching out, Troy shoved him in the shoulder. "Hey, man, cool it. You're here to help me find a killer, not punish him. That's up to the law. Understand?"

Mike shot him a vicious look. "If Pete had been your brother, you'd waste the guy quicker than blinking an eye!" he growled. "Don't pretend you wouldn't, man!"

Troy shook his head. "No. I'd drag him kicking and screaming to court. I'd make sure he got a proper trial.

Then I'd enjoy every day he rotted in some stinking prison cell."

Slowly, the tension drained from Mike's face. "Yeah. I could dig that too."

Jennifer had a lot on her mind, and none of it was good.

She'd reported for work at noon and since then had watched Troy hobble a dozen times on his bad leg back and forth in front of Caramelbun. She didn't know what he was up to, but figured it must have something to do with his investigation for the sheriff.

From the stiff strides he took, she could tell he was in pain. Every step must have pulled against the stitches in his thigh. His dedication to his job made her like him even more.

Unfortunately, he'd already told her good-bye . . . or at least that they could never have a romantic relationship. His only reason for being in McCarter was to help hunt down a murderer. Once he'd found that person he would leave, and she'd never see him again.

Jennifer swallowed over a raw spot in her throat. Why did falling in love have to hurt so much?

Fortunately, she didn't have time to be miserable. Business at Caramelbun was unusually brisk and got positively crazy around six o'clock.

"Can you take your break a little later?" Jerry asked.

"Sure," Jennifer agreed. She didn't care if she ever ate again. She'd permanently lost her appetite.

Due to an advertised special, each customer who ordered a dozen buns received a free liter of soda. By eight o'clock, the line in front of Caramelbun was still long. Jennifer nibbled on broken pieces of sweet rolls and sipped chocolate milk out of a carton to keep up her energy.

It was close to nine when business finally slacked off and Jerry tapped her on the shoulder. "I'll take over.

You can go home early since you didn't get dinner tonight."

"I'm fine," she told him, although her eyes burned and the backs of her legs ached from standing for six hours straight.

"You look like hell," he said sympathetically. "Get some sleep. You're scheduled to work after tennis team tomorrow."

Jennifer took a deep breath and nodded. She walked away in a daze, bumping into shoppers as she crossed the mall, oblivious to everything around her. She had almost reached the arcade when she became aware of someone calling her name.

"Hey, Jen! Wait up!"

She stopped dead in her tracks and closed her eyes for a moment, trying to control the surge of anger, for she'd immediately recognized the voice.

"Jen? Is something wrong?" Patty asked breathlessly, running up to her.

"Yes-s-s . . . something is wrong," Jennifer hissed between her teeth. Last night, Jennifer hadn't slept more than a couple hours because after she'd stopped worrying about Troy, all she could think about was that her very best friend in the world was a thief. To make matters worse, not only had Patty stolen an expensive dress, she'd tricked Jennifer into helping her, which was unforgivable.

Patty frowned at her, puzzled. "Well? So tell already."

"*You!*" Jennifer snapped, starting to walk again.

Patty jogged to keep up with her. "*Me?* What have I done?"

"You conned me into helping you steal."

"I *what?*" Patty gasped.

"You know very well what you did," Jennifer snapped. "You stole that two-hundred-dollar dress, then talked me into stashing it in my car so you wouldn't get caught with it."

Patty seized her arm, forcing her to stop in the middle of the crowded mall. "What are you talking about?" she demanded in a hoarse whisper, looking around to make sure no one had heard Jennifer's accusation. "I didn't steal anything!"

"Yeah, sure. Like you had two hundred dollars—"

"Two-fifty," Patty corrected.

"Whatever! Two-fifty hanging around in your purse."

"No, I didn't," Patty began, her eyes narrowing. "There are other ways to get something if you really want it."

"Well, I resent your involving *me* in your little schemes!" Jennifer said. "Friends don't use friends."

Patty opened her mouth to respond, but, just then, Louise stepped between them.

"Hi," she said meekly. "I—uh—hope I'm not interrupting anything but . . . well, I was just wondering if either of you know what Troy and Mike Foley are up to?"

"Huh?" Jennifer and Patty chorused.

"A little while ago I saw them head toward the rear section of Books N Things. I waited for them to come back past the desk. I wanted to ask Troy if he was okay . . . cause I noticed he was limping something awful. But I never saw him and Mike come out through the store."

Jennifer blinked, confused. "They must have just slipped past when you were busy."

"No," Louise insisted. "I see everything."

Jennifer hesitated. She couldn't tell either of the other girls that Troy was working for the sheriff. She'd promised.

"Troy's business is his own," she said coolly. "I'm not interested in what he does. I don't see why you should be."

Louise and Patty exchanged knowing glances.

"I heard you were dating him," Louise said.

"So? I heard you went out with Ben Derby. What's the big deal?"

"Nothing," Louise said defensively. "I just thought you might know what was going on. So much weird stuff is happening around here these days."

A faint alarm sounded in Jennifer's brain. "Like what?" she asked.

Louise shrugged. "A lot. For instance . . . at your father's store. When I leave at night, and sometimes that's pretty late, someone's often still in SuperCharged. Usually it's Gary."

"He's a hard worker," Jennifer said.

"Maybe. But he's awfully nervous. I went over there once, to ask if he needed help closing or something. He nearly chased me out of the store. I think he's hiding something."

Jennifer scowled, considering this. When Troy had been hurt last night, Gary was still around.

"And those strange people who come here every night . . ." Louise shook her head.

"The homeless couple?" Jennifer asked.

"They aren't exactly homeless," Louise said mysteriously.

"Oh, sure. Like they'd be hiding out in the mall every night if they had a cozy apartment on San Jacinto Street," Patty muttered skeptically.

"The mall *is* their home," Louise explained.

"What?" Jennifer asked.

"Sure. They have a room all set up behind the bookstore. I discovered it a long time ago, but didn't say anything. I didn't want to get them in trouble."

"Oh, geez," Patty breathed. "I bet they want to keep their place secret. Do you think they'd be desperate enough to kill someone to keep it to themselves?"

"You mean . . . they might have killed Eleanor? Their

friend?" Patty and Louise hadn't made the connection between Pete Foley and the mall . . . and Jennifer couldn't talk about that without explaining about Troy.

"Who knows. Maybe they had a fight," Patty suggested. "Maybe old Eleanor did something that threatened to give them away. Then you stumbled on their hiding place that night when you were taking the back way out to the parking lot—"

"I wasn't on that side of the mall," Jennifer reminded her. "I was behind SuperCharged when—" She blinked, blinked again . . . it was coming back to her.

A slow, reptilian chill climbed her spine, and she gasped, "Oh, God!"

"What?" Patty demanded.

"It's Gary . . . he was here last night when Troy got hurt. He must have been at SuperCharged that night I tried to leave by the back way."

"Gary Pyzik tried to kill you?" Patty choked out. "That's insane! He's a wimp! He has no motive!"

"He's stealing stuff from SuperCharged. My dad's lost thousands of dollars in merchandise to shoplifters, or so he thought. Gary must have been loading stuff into the back of his truck when I came along and surprised him."

"Just like Eleanor." Louise shook her head sadly. "Poor old lady."

And just like Pete Foley, who must have come by the mall the night he died, Jennifer thought. They'd all seen something . . . something that could put Gary away for a long, long time.

Jennifer spun around and charged into Books N Things.

"Where are you going?" Louise called after her.

"I have to warn Troy!"

By the time Jennifer reached the back of the bookstore, Louise and Patty were only a few steps behind her. "Is the secret room back through here?" Jennifer asked, lifting the curtain and peering into the dim storage area.

"Yes, behind that wall of empty boxes." Louise stepped forward.

"No," Jennifer said quickly, blocking the other girls with one arm. "You two stay here. If anyone who doesn't work in the bookstore tries to go through this door, stop them. If you can't, call the sheriff's office."

"What do I say?" Louise asked.

"Tell him Troy is in trouble. He'll understand."

Chapter 13

TROY AND MIKE sat with their backs to the wall, one on each side of the doorway in the secret room. The minutes ticked past slowly. They didn't dare talk for fear of warning their prey before they could close their trap.

Troy took out the .45 automatic. In the dark, by touch, he loaded a clip and clicked the safety to the off position. He slid the gun back into the shoulder holster.

Troy knew how to use the gun, although he hoped he wouldn't have to. Sheriff Patterson had registered it for him and given it to him after checking him out on the firing range.

"Just in case," had been the sheriff's words.

But if the man and woman they were lying in wait for became violent, Troy might have no choice.

At last a soft scuffling issued through the tunnel. It was no louder than the sound of a sheet of paper being blown across a room. Nothing that would have ordinarily captured his interest. But tonight subtle sounds meant danger. Troy changed his mind, reached beneath his shirt, and pulled out the .45 to hold in his hand.

He'd instructed Mike to make no move and say nothing until he did. True to his word, Mike was remaining perfectly still on his side of the doorway. Troy couldn't tell if he too had heard the muffled movements in the tunnel, but he didn't dare risk speaking now. As he silently drew up his knees, ready to spring to his feet, his stitches pulled painfully.

Suddenly sensing a presence in the doorway, Troy held his breath. No one was visible in the blackness. No one made a sound. But he could feel someone's presence, and the hairs on the back of his neck stood at alert. *They're listening,* he thought, *making sure their home hasn't been invaded.*

Finally, one set of catlike footsteps hastily crossed the room.

I want you both! Troy thought grimly, determined to make the trap perfect. He might get the one who knew nothing and miss the other who could have told him what he needed to know.

Then a surprisingly clear voice announced, "I'll set the table."

The lamp flickered on, and the room was filled with light.

Troy and Mike stood on either side of the doorway, blinking at the sudden brightness. A man and woman in rumpled clothing stared at them in shock. The woman's eyes fixed fearfully on the gun in Troy's hand.

"Get out!" growled the man. "Go away!"

Troy shook his head. "Two people have been killed in the mall, or near it. Another almost died. I'm here to find out who was responsible."

"We never hurt no one," the young woman responded quickly, her voice taut.

"I didn't accuse either of you of hurting anyone. I just need information."

"Get out of here!" the man ordered again. He might easily have been sixty or more years old. His hair and the longish stubble of his beard was steely gray. "We don't bother anyone," he added.

"You seem to have bothered some people's property, though," Troy pointed out. "I could arrest you for swiping this stuff from the stores."

"It's all junk," the woman pleaded, tears glistening in her eyes. "We only take things no one wants. Damaged things they can't sell. Garbage. See the table?" She pointed to one corner where the finish was completed chipped away.

"I need information," Troy insisted, feeling Mike's frustration from a few feet behind him. Troy stepped toward the man and motioned with his gun. "Sit down. We have to talk."

But the man didn't move. "I have nothing to say. Neither does Alice. We don't hurt people. We don't take nothing they can use. All we want is a safe place to sleep until times get better."

"Now we'll have to move," Alice whimpered. "You'll tell people we're here. They'll come and yell at us and kick us out of our room."

The man's eyes darkened and grew defiant. "We aren't saying anything. We don't know anything. Go away."

Troy looked at Mike. The other boy was tensed to throw himself on the guy. Troy stepped between the two and turned to Mike. "No, man. You can't do that."

"They *know!*" Mike yelled. "Any idiot can tell they're lying! They know what happened to Pete!" He screamed over Troy's shoulder at the man, "You bastard, what did you do to my brother?"

It was at that moment that Jennifer burst into the room. Breathing raggedly, she looked around as if she were a school teacher on a field trip, counting heads to make sure she had everyone.

"What's going on?" she rasped out.

"Go away, Jen," Troy said without taking his eyes off of the old man. "You don't belong here."

"No," she said firmly. "I have to tell you something important."

"It can wait. Go!" Troy barked out.

Jennifer shook her head stubbornly. "These people didn't do anything. Gary Pyzik is behind the murders."

Troy shot a worried look at Mike. The boy was close to snapping. "I suspect you're right," Troy muttered.

"But we need proof. We need witnesses." He spoke directly to the man and woman in front of him. "You have to help us."

The woman licked her lips and glanced at the man. He shook his head, and she closed her mouth firmly.

"Troy," Jennifer said, "put the gun away. You're scaring them to death." She turned away from him and spoke to the two strangers. "Listen, I don't know either of you, but I have a feeling you've seen me before."

They stared at her in silence.

"I almost didn't make it." Reaching up, she pulled the collar of her shirt down to reveal the ugly scar around her throat.

The woman gasped aloud. "You! He didn't kill—" She slapped a hand over her own mouth.

"Shut up!" the man ordered. "She's trying to trick you."

"*This* could happen to you," Jennifer persisted. "Only next time there might be no one to stop him! Did you call for the ambulance? Did you scare Gary off? If you did, you saved my life."

"Oh, Joshua!" The woman wailed. "I can't. I can't just . . . just do nothing!"

Jennifer glanced sideways at Troy. He seemed to realize she was getting further with the couple than he had and was letting her continue. Carefully, he tucked the gun back beneath his shirt.

"What happened that night?" Jennifer whispered.

"I saw him . . . we both did. He had you around the throat with a long strip of plastic packaging cord. But I didn't tell no one. I was too afraid," Alice admitted. She glanced at her companion. "Joshua said if I called the police, they'd think I did it. Just like with poor Eleanor. After she was killed, one of the newspapers said we murdered her . . . a squabble over food, they said. But there's always plenty of food at the mall that gets thrown away every day. Besides," she added sadly, "we were friends, the three of us."

"What happened to her?" Jennifer asked.

"It was all very . . . very confusing." The woman broke into jagged sobs.

Joshua stepped forward, his eyes hollow, his bravado suddenly deflated. "Alice didn't see much. It was me that was there right after it happened."

"You saw who it was?" Jennifer asked.

"I didn't see him do it. Just saw him standing over her. That young man from the electronics store."

"Gary," Troy breathed.

"He had a rope or something in his hands, and he was standing over her. But she was already gone. There was nothing I could do."

"Where were they?" Jennifer asked.

"Behind the electronics store, near the loading dock. We saw him there a lot. We knew what he was up to . . . stealing stuff from his own store—"

"My father's store," Jennifer spat out, anger boiling up inside her. "Did he see you?"

"No," Joshua said. "I don't think he did . . . that time." He looked at her with meaning.

"You mean, he saw you watching him another time? When he killed Pete Foley?"

"We read about that in the paper." Alice sniffled. "That poor boy, they said he hanged himself. But *I* don't think he did."

Joshua explained. "After we saw the newspaper articles, we remembered noticing the boy behind the mall, arguing with someone on the loading dock. I guess he must have known something funny was going on."

Jennifer let out a long breath. "Thank you," she murmured, then looked at Troy. "What now?"

"I report all of this to the sheriff. He has to determine the next move." He glanced at Mike. "I can read your mind, man. You want to tear out of here and hunt down Gary. Don't do it."

"Give me one reason why I shouldn't," Mike demanded tightly.

"He might get away. He's pretty smart, you know. He rigged that elevator."

"How'd he do that?" Jennifer asked.

"We can't be sure until an electronics expert verifies it, but I'd bet any money that Gary rebuilt the TV remote control he was holding to function as a remote device for the elevator. He waited until I was in the shaft and you were clear, then hit the button."

Jennifer recalled Gary reaching for the remote control in his pocket just before the elevator descended on Troy. She shut her eyes, feeling sick to her stomach at the thought.

"My father will feel responsible," she said softly. "He hired Gary. He trusted him."

"It's not his fault. He had no idea what the guy was up to." Troy paused, frowning.

"What's wrong?" Jennifer asked.

"I don't know . . . nothing," he decided quickly. "Just a loose end I can't quite figure." He looked at Joshua. "Will you and Alice tell the sheriff what you told us?"

Joshua avoided Troy's eyes. "We don't want to get involved. We just want to be left alone. If we tell your sheriff, he'll want us to make a statement in a courtroom. Everyone will ask questions about us. We'll lose our home. We've already lost too much," he said sadly.

"But . . . but you have to—" Troy stammered urgently, "you're our only witnesses. I swear, no one's going to chase you away from here. And the sheriff will protect you."

The old man gazed at him thoughtfully.

Jennifer touched Troy on the arm. "Let's go now. I

think Joshua and Alice have told us everything they can for now."

He looked at her, trying to read the hidden message beneath her words.

A few minutes later, Jennifer, Troy, and Mike emerged from behind the storage room curtain, into the brightly lit bookstore. Patty and Louise rushed at them.

"What's going on?" Patty demanded.

Louise pushed her out of the way. "Did you find them? Did they talk to you?"

Troy glared at Jennifer. "What are these two doing here?"

"They were my backup . . . in case someone tried to follow me. They don't know about . . . you know." She had to reassure Troy that she hadn't give away his identity.

He nodded, understanding.

"We don't know about what?" Patty asked, her eyes huge with curiosity.

"You'll have to wait," Jennifer told her. "It will all be over soon."

Chapter 14

To Troy, Loy Patterson looked like a man who should wear boots on his feet and a star on his chest. The sheriff was tall and muscular, with the patience and long liquid drawl of a Texan. He listened to Troy's description of Joshua and Alice and every word of what they'd told him without interrupting once.

Troy was careful to leave out nothing of what they'd said. But he intentionally omitted the fact that Mike and Jennifer had been with him in the tiny room behind the bookstore. If Patterson had asked if anyone else had been there, he'd have told him. But he didn't, so Troy decided not to bring it up; he sensed the lawman wouldn't approve of him involving civilians.

"You believe their story?" Patterson asked when Troy finished.

"Yes," he replied carefully. "Everything fits. For over a year Gary Pyzik has been stealing electronics equipment from SuperCharged. To get caught would mean the end of all his plans for the future. He wouldn't graduate from high school, or go to college. He'd spend time in prison, be released with a record and have a hell of a time getting a job because of it. From what the other kids have told me, Gary's a very ambitious kid. In his rush to succeed, I think he made some bad decisions."

"You think Pete Foley was a threat to him," the sheriff stated thoughtfully.

"Right. Pete walked his date home from the movies

that night, then started back to his own house. On the way, he took a shortcut across the mall parking lot. That's where the Boylestons spotted him. Then, as he came around the back of the mall, Pete must have noticed a light at the loading dock."

"He realized what was going on and tried to stop Mr. Pyzik from putting merchandise on his truck?"

"Probably not right away," Troy guessed, imagining how it might have been that night. "More likely, Pete was just at the wrong place at the wrong time. He might have been tired of walking, recognized Gary's truck, and decided to ask for a ride."

The sheriff nodded. "Sounds logical. But once he saw the stuff in the truck, he'd put two and two together."

"Exactly," Troy said. "Pete tried to leave, but Gary couldn't afford to let him. They struggled, and Gary choked Pete to death. Gary had to think fast. He came up with the idea of faking a suicide to cover the murder."

"What about the note? We verified that the handwriting was Pete's," pointed out the sheriff.

"When you showed it to me, I noticed that it was written on a torn piece of notebook paper. Kids are always writing notes to their friends in school. If Gary found an old letter in Pete's pocket, he could have chosen the part he wanted to use and thrown away the rest. Remember what the note said?"

" 'Can't deal with this any more,' " Patterson recited.

"Well," Troy said, "couldn't that mean a lot of things? He was saying so-long to his old girlfriend, or he was complaining about how tough one of his classes was, or telling a buddy that his crazy brother was driving him up a wall. It doesn't have to mean he was ready to shut out the lights forever!"

"Good thinking," Patterson commented, allowing Troy his first smile of the night. "Then six months later, this Gary fella is threatened again when old Eleanor sees him making off with goods from the electronics store. And it was the same way with little Jennifer. How long does this guy think he can go on wiping people out without someone getting wise to him?"

Troy shook his head. He didn't understand that either. *Little Jennifer,* he thought, a warm glow filling his chest. For some reason, she had been different. Why hadn't Gary finished her off? After all, it was either her or his entire future. Had he stopped because Joshua and Alice came along? And what about the garrote in the elevator shaft? Had Gary planted it there, knowing Troy would go after it? Something didn't quite make sense.

"Well," Sheriff Patterson interrupted his thoughts as he stood behind the gray metal desk and stretched his arms high over his head. "Guess we'd better get a coupla men and a car."

Troy stared at him, puzzled. "You mean, we can pick up Gary on just what we have?"

Patterson laughed. "Of course not, son. All of this is pure conjecture . . . words in the air. But once we bring in those two vagrants and get sworn statements from them, then we'll have something."

Troy jumped up, alarmed. "You can't . . . I mean, I don't think they'll testify in court. They're scared to death!"

"I don't care how loud their teeth chatter while they spill their story," Patterson said tightly. "The bottom line is, they're gonna talk because we got no case without them. Now, you lead us to that secret room of theirs, then go on to the motel and catch a few hours sleep. I want you back at the mall before Mr. Pyzik arrives for his after-school job."

"What do I do?"

"Keep an eye on him. I want to know where he is every minute of the day. I'll have two men watch his house tonight and tail him to school. Once he's at the mall, he's yours. But don't do anything to spook him. Understand? If he thinks we're on to him, he might cut out.''

"What will happen to Joshua and Alice?" Troy asked weakly. "I promised we wouldn't chase them out of their room."

"You shouldn't have done that, son. I can't leave them there. It's private property, belongs to Mall Management. And anyway, they won't be able to go back to the mall for a good while. I'll have to keep them in protective custody until the trial, to make sure they don't skip town."

"Oh," Troy mumbled miserably. He'd promised Joshua that they'd be safe.

But he had no choice if he wanted to catch his murderer—the first of his career. Besides, not until Gary was behind bars would Jennifer be safe.

He rode in the sheriff's car. Two deputies, weighed down with enough fire power to take a small town, followed in a second cruiser. Troy used the driving time to think over everything he'd learned about McCarter Mall in the last few months. Something still didn't make sense. If he could only put his finger on what that was . . .

For instance, if Gary had intended to kill Jennifer and he had rigged the elevator to fall on his command, why hadn't Gary pushed *her* into the shaft as soon as he, Troy, jumped in? That certainly would have guaranteed they'd both be crushed to death and would no longer pose a threat to him. In fact, as Gary had run toward them that night, he had made every effort to steer Jennifer away from the sabotaged machine.

Unfortunately, Troy had no more time to dwell on details. The two cruisers pulled silently up to the security entrance of the mall, headlights dimmed, sirens silent to avoid alarming Joshua and Alice. After obtaining the bookstore's keys from the guard on duty, the four men ran noiselessly through the deserted mall.

Books N Things was diagonally across the corridor from SuperCharged. Troy stared at the windows while one of the other deputies worked the lock on the folding metal grate that slid across the front of the bookstore. The electronics store's windows were dark; nothing moved behind them. Within seconds the deputy had the grate open and they were running through the store.

Troy pointed out the curtained doorway. "The room's through here," he whispered, reluctantly.

"You lead the way." Patterson handed him a high-powered flashlight.

Slowly, Troy moved into the store room, then the narrow hallway beyond. The flashlight illuminated the cement walls, casting monstrous black shadows. *One thing's for sure,* Troy thought wryly, *we won't take Joshua and Alice by surprise.*

At the end of the tunnel he could see the dark doorways of the two rooms. Patterson tapped Troy on the shoulder. "Which one?" he mouthed.

"The left," Troy said.

The two deputies moved ahead on signal from the sheriff, assault rifles raised. Patterson took the flashlight from Troy and waved him back, but he followed anyway. Since he'd betrayed Joshua, the least he could do was be there to confront him. His heart raced in his chest. *Don't hurt them,* he prayed. *They don't mean any harm.*

"Freeze!" one of the deputies barked as he suddenly leaped into the room.

The others rushed in after him.

For several seconds all four intruders stared around the room. Patterson moved the flashlight about, and Troy noticed that the blankets, food, and spare clothing were missing. Only the borrowed furniture remained.

"They've gone . . . cleared out," Troy said, hiding a

smile. *You're smart, Joshua. You knew we couldn't leave you alone.*

But a terrible coldness closed around his heart. For with Joshua and Alice out of the picture, there were no witnesses. No one and nothing remained to tie together shreds of evidence against a killer.

Jennifer thought about Troy all day through her classes. In first period she hated him for tricking her into thinking he was someone he wasn't. In second her heart softened, and she decided she adored him because he had saved her life. By the time Independent Studies rolled around, she was furious with him for shutting her out of his life.

But when she walked onto the courts for tennis team after school, her emotions had stabilized, and she admitted to herself that she was going to miss him when he left McCarter. Before that lonely day, she wanted to see him again to thank him for saving her life, and caring about her . . . if only as a friend.

"How's the new backhand coming?"

Jennifer snapped out of her daze and looked across the net at Ben Derby. "Okay, I guess."

"Want me to hit to you?"

"Sure," she said without much enthusiasm.

Ben repeatedly sent balls to her left side, forcing her to return each shot with a backhand. She gripped the racquet with both hands, hitting up and through the ball and ending each swing with the racquet edge pointing straight up in front of her nose to make the ball dive crisply over the net.

"Good," Ben said. "It's coming along. You still going out with that security guard?"

"No!" Jennifer smashed the next ball.

It zoomed over the net and took a fierce bounce an inch from Ben's feet, making it impossible for him to return the shot.

"Nice aggressive stroke," he commented, hiding a smile.

"You still dating Louise?" she asked.

"Not really."

"Why not?" Everyone's love life couldn't be as messed up as hers.

He shrugged and lobbed a half-hearted shot to her. "She found out I was seeing some chick in Houston on the side."

Jennifer jammed her fists down on her hips and glared at Ben, ignoring the ball as it bounced past. "You mean you two were going together and you . . . you . . . How could you, Derby?"

"Old habits die hard." He sighed and walked dejectedly toward the net. "Hey, I admit that I blew it. Louise is the nicest girl I've ever dated. I'd go back with her and try again. But she won't even talk to me."

"Serves you right." She took in his puppy dog eyes and felt sorry for him. "Sorry, I warned you."

"Yeah." He cleared his throat, blinking at the setting sun. "I've been thinking. Maybe I'll take a break from girls for a while. You know, work on my tennis game, catch up on homework, sign on for a few extra hours at Burger Delite. Maybe Louise will cool down if she sees I've changed my ways."

"Then what?"

"I don't know. I should have some extra cash saved up by then. I could ask her to Homecoming, take her somewhere really special for dinner before the dance. Think she'd go with me?"

"Only one way to find out—ask," Jennifer said, patting him on the back. "Good luck."

She felt better after her conversation with Ben. As soon as the coach dismissed practice, she decided to go and see Troy. She drove to the motel and knocked on his door. He didn't answer. Although she had another hour before she needed to report for work, she went straight to the mall, hoping to find him there.

Troy was standing in front of Books N Things, a paperback novel open in one hand. But his eyes were directed at the bookstore's display window, which reflected the entrance to SuperCharged.

"On a stakeout?" Jennifer whispered from behind.

Troy hid his surprise except for a telltale twinge in the muscle at the back of his neck. "What are you doing here?" he asked stiffly.

"I work in the mall, remember?"

"You should go home. Tell your boss you're sick."

"I don't want to," she said sweetly.

"Listen, Jen." He turned to her, his gray eyes solemn. "I admit that you helped out last night. I don't think Joshua and Alice would have told me anything if you hadn't come along. But you can't hang around now. It's too dangerous. Gary's going to screw up sooner or later, and when he does I don't want anyone hanging around to get hurt."

Jennifer considered this for a minute. "If he's so dangerous, then anyone in a position to figure out what he's been doing is at risk. Right? He could kill again."

"You've got it."

"Then I think the sheriff should tell my father what's going on. He works with Gary. SuperCharged is his store."

She caught a glimpse of Gary through the showcase window of her father's store. Never would she have thought such a quiet boy could be a murderer. Never. But she supposed that was why sickos got away with killing people. No one really knew what another person was capable of—what evil lurked in someone else's soul.

Troy cleared his throat. "Sheriff Patterson says no one else is to know about Gary, for now. The fewer people who do, the better our chances of catching him. He's clever enough to sense a trap if everyone around him is in on it."

Jennifer took a deep breath, fixing her eyes on Troy's darker ones. "I understand," she said stiffly. But she didn't say that she agreed.

Troy reached out to gently touch her fingertips, then the base of her throat, as if reminding himself how close he'd come to losing her once before.

"So long, Jen," he whispered. "Have a good life."

Jennifer could hardly see her way through the crowd. Tears filled her eyes. Angrily, she wiped them away on the sleeve of her blouse. Troy had said good-bye to her. Although she knew that it had been coming, she'd been unprepared for it to happen so quickly. Her insides ached. She felt empty and alone.

It was because of the tears and her haste to get away from the place where she'd stood with Troy that she ran straight into Louise. The girl looked relieved to see her and immediately pulled her to the edge of the crowd.

"They're gone!" Louise hissed in her ear.

"Who's gone?"

"The two people who were living in back of the bookstore. I checked the room this morning. They've taken most of their stuff."

So that was why Troy was so tense. He'd lost his witnesses. Jennifer wondered what had frightened Joshua and Alice enough to make them leave their cozy adopted home.

Suddenly, she felt as if someone were watching her. She turned around, but saw only a constant flow of ordinary shoppers. The holiday bargain hunters were already out. In a couple of weeks, Santa would be seated in a plastic ice-block chair beside the fountain, bouncing little kids on his knee and asking if they'd been good all year.

The cheery image made her want to make someone

happy, even though she was sure it would take her a long time to get over Troy and be happy herself.

"I saw Ben Derby today," she said.

Louise stiffened. "So?"

"Do you still like him?" Jennifer asked.

"I've learned my lesson," Louise evaded the question.

"I think, if you gave him another chance you might be surprised," Jennifer suggested. "He's a sheep hiding inside a wolf's skin."

"Huh?"

"He's really a good guy making like a jerk. I think he's figured that out."

Shaking her head doubtfully, Louise pushed her glasses up the bridge of her nose and peered at Jennifer through the thick lenses. "I think I'm better off on my own."

Chapter 15

THAT NIGHT, JENNIFER made 535 caramel buns before six o'clock. However, eight of them didn't really count. Her nervous energy demanded sugar and she gave in to her craving. She ate one after another as soon as they came out of the oven, hot, sweet, and gooey.

For some reason, the food cleared her head. She decided that Troy was only doing what he had to do—following orders to trap a killer. Well, she had an obligation too.

All of her eighteen years her father had played an important role in her life. He might have been a workaholic. He might have been strict, sometimes irrationally strict, and they hadn't always gotten along. But she had no doubt that every rule he made had been for her own good, at least in his mind. Now it was up to her protect him, even if by doing so she ignored Troy's warning.

She shoved a huge pan of buns into the industrial-size oven, shut the door, then reached for the telephone and dialed.

"Good evening, SuperCharged! How may I help you?"

It was Gary. She almost dropped the receiver but took a deep breath and forced her voice to remain calm.

"Hi, Gary, is my dad there?"

"Oh, Jennifer . . . sure. Hold on."

A second later her father came on the line. "Listen,

sweetheart, things are really busy tonight. Can I call you back?"

"Wait!" she gasped before he could hang up. "I just wanted to ask you to have supper with me."

"Let's do it another time," he suggested.

"No," Jennifer answered firmly. "I need to talk to you right away." She lowered her voice. "It has to do with the person who attacked me. I know who he was."

There was a moment's hesitation then, "The Beef Pit," her father said. "I'll meet you there at seven-thirty."

Jennifer arrived a few minutes early at the new restaurant that had been built across the parking lot from the mall. It was a popular place to take a date for a casual dinner. She walked up wooden steps into a lobby decorated with saddles, spurs, bridles, and a stuffed dead horse named Clyde. Her father was waiting for her.

"I thought about meeting you at Caramelbun and walking you over," he said anxiously. "I hadn't realized it would be this dark yet."

"It's okay," she said. "I drove."

"Oh—"

He looked distracted, as if his mind was in a hundred other places. His dark hair, the same deep black as hers, receded sharply at the forehead. It contrasted vividly with the chalky skin of his scalp and cheeks. *You work too hard, Dad,* she thought.

"Table for two," he told the hostess. "Nonsmoking . . . somewhere quiet."

"Yes, sir." The girl led them to seats at the very back of the restaurant, away from other occupied tables.

Jennifer was glad they could talk openly without being overheard. She wasn't sure how her father would react to the news about Gary.

They ordered. Jennifer, a bacon cheeseburger and fries. Her father a rare T-bone steak with baked potato and spinach salad.

"Hungry, huh?" she asked, trying to make conversation.

"Excuse me?"

"The steak. That's a big meal for a working night. You usually just grab a slice of pizza or a chicken sandwich."

"Oh—I wasn't thinking much about the food. The steak was the first thing on the menu."

He took a drink of water, his hands trembling, and she felt sorry for him. Her brush with death must have been even harder on him than she'd realized.

"So," he began, "what do you have to tell me about this creep who came after you? Who do you think he was?"

She looked solemnly across the table at him in the dim light. "It's not who I *think* he was . . . it's who I *know* he was," she said with emphasis. "And I wasn't his first target. He's actually killed two people. Pete Foley, the boy from my school who supposedly committed suicide, and Eleanor Duvall, the old woman who was found dead at the mall last April."

Her father's eyes narrowed. "How did you come up with this crazy idea, Jennifer?"

"It isn't crazy. The sheriff's office has been working on these cases, on the theory that they're somehow linked."

"And who told you this?"

"Troy."

"The security guard you wanted to date?" He was watching her intently, the way he'd done when she broke the terrible news to him that she wasn't going to make honor's list one quarter in her sophomore year.

"Yes," she said, choosing her words carefully. "Troy found out that Gary Pyzik was responsible for both deaths as well as for strangling me. Gary has been stealing from your store for a long time. When Pete and later Eleanor caught him in the act, he was desperate to keep them from telling anyone. Apparently there was only one way to make sure they wouldn't talk."

Her father's eyes darkened still more, burrowing into hers. "You're certain about this? They're positive that it's Gary? He was working alone?"

"Yes," she said regretfully. "I know this must be a terrible shock to you, Dad. You hired him and he's worked so closely with you the last couple of years . . . But the important thing is, you can't let on to Gary that you know anything. The sheriff still has to wind up the investigation."

Their meals arrived. Jennifer dove into her cheeseburger, feeling better now that she'd warned her father. But he played with his steak, cutting it into little chunks, then pushing them around the plate with his fork while lost in thought.

At last Jennifer caught his eye across the table. "I think you should stay away from the store for a while," she suggested. "The sheriff's office has staked out SuperCharged. If Gary figures out what's going on, he might do something off the wall. He's dangerous, Dad. He tried to kill Troy by tampering with the elevator."

Looking troubled, Mr. Merrill put down his fork. "Why haven't they arrested him?"

"Because they have no solid proof. Everything is based on piecing together dates, times, and a couple statements. But the only real witnesses are two homeless friends of old Eleanor, who have disappeared. So now the sheriff has to dig up enough evidence to convict Gary."

Her father shook his head. "Building an airtight case might take a long time. If Gary was careful when he rewired that elevator, he didn't leave fingerprints."

Something in her father's words jangled a nerve in Jennifer's brain. She scowled, wondering what it had been that alarmed her.

"I suppose so," she said slowly. "But I'd still feel better if you took a vacation until this was all over."

Her father sighed, looking at her hard. "I can't stay away from the store, because that would be unusual behavior for me, which might tip Gary off that the police are on to him."

Jennifer clenched her fists in her lap. "But, Dad—"

"No arguing. I know what's best. *I* stay, but *you* go." He continued before she could object, "I'm withdrawing permission for you to work at the mall. You are to go straight home from here. I'll call your manager and let him know that you won't be back tonight or until further notice, due to a family emergency."

"What emergency is that?" she demanded.

"Your safety," he said shortly. He tossed his napkin on the tabletop and signalled the waitress for the check, even though he'd finished less than half of his steak.

"Dad," she pleaded. "If I thought you'd wig out like this, I wouldn't have told you anything."

He kissed her hastily on the forehead as he stood up. "You were looking out for your old man. I'm proud of you and appreciate your concern. You're a good girl. Now go home, Jennifer Ann."

Jennifer sat in her car, parked in front of her house. Everything was going wrong! Troy had asked her to tell no one who he was or about Gary's guilt. She'd spilled everything to her father, and it had done absolutely no good. He was still in danger.

She didn't want to go inside, but she had no choice. Her father's word was law in their home. Besides, if she went back to the mall and ran into Troy . . . how could she ever face him? She dried her tears and climbed out of the Miata.

As soon as she stepped through the door her mother's voice echoed down the stairway from the master bedroom suite. "Is that you, Jennifer?"

"It's me," she responded in a brittle, plastic voice. Her head ached miserably, and an awful sensation in the pit of her stomach warned her that something bad was brewing.

She wasn't afraid for herself. But she was terrified for

all the people in her life who might get hurt. Her father—working in the same store with a murderer. Her mother—she'd never had a job outside of their home. What would she do if anything happened to her husband? And Troy . . . wonderful Troy. If it came down to a face-off with Gary, would he survive?

She climbed the stairs to her bedroom, trembling. Her whole world was crumbling around her.

Jennifer lay down on her bed in the dark and touched her throat, tears seeping between her shut lids. So close to death . . . so close she'd come. If it hadn't been for someone who'd cared enough to stop Gary . . .

Her eyes sprang open as she heard in her imagination the voice that had called her name that night.

"Jennifer . . . Oh, God, Jennifer!"

That voice had brought her back from the precipice of death. A man's voice. But not Gary's high-pitched, nervous twang. And not Troy's smooth Texas drawl. Which left only one other person, as incredible as it seemed, who had any reason to be in the loading dock area that night, and who would be that upset about her dying.

She sat up on the bed, shaking from her fingernails to the tips of her toes. Her stomach curdled and clenched with horror at the awful truth.

If *her father,* not Gary, had been the brains behind the thefts, he would have a great deal to lose by being discovered. What if he hadn't recognized the person who'd surprised him in the loading dock tunnel? He'd seen a moving figure, knew it was only a matter of seconds before the intruder spotted the equipment he was loading into Gary's truck, came up behind with a knotted length of packaging twine . . . But only when she'd slumped, unconscious, to the floor had he seen her face and loosened the band around her throat!

Jennifer's mind raced now, plucking facts from the air. Amazingly, so much seemed to make sense now. The unusual number of thefts from SuperCharged . . .

Pete's death . . . Her father had worked that night. She remembered because he'd slept late the next morning to make up for the late hour, which was very unusual for him. And she'd seen the ambulance and sheriff's cars on the football field that morning.

And then she realized what had alarmed her in the restaurant. Her father had remarked that Gary must have been careful to leave no fingerprints *when he'd rewired the elevator.* But she was certain she'd told her father nothing about how the elevator had been rigged. She'd only said that Gary had tampered with it. Her father had supplied the rest . . . because he knew . . . *because he was the electronics expert and he'd shown Gary how to do it!*

Jennifer clutched her stomach and dashed for the bathroom. After a couple minutes of dry heaves over the toilet, she leaned back against the cold, tile wall and wiped tears from her burning cheeks. Gulping to catch her breath, she forced everything from her mind except her memory of the night she'd been attacked. Once she was unconscious at her father's feet, he would have been able to do little to help her without incriminating himself. He must have cleared away evidence of the thefts, telephoned anonymously for an ambulance, then quickly driven home to wait for the call from the hospital.

Jennifer grabbed hold of the sink and dragged herself to her feet. Feeling as if a part of her had died, she staggered back into the bedroom and seized her purse. She was sure that her father had sent her home because he was planning one last desperate act to get himself off the hook.

Somehow she had to warn Troy.

Troy made himself as inconspicuous as possible. He wandered in SuperCharged only twice during the evening, giving Gary a quick wave while making a show of checking out the customers. It was nothing more or less than he'd normally do while on the job. The rest of the evening while he watched the storefront, he made sure he wasn't visible from the cashier's desk where Gary often stood ringing up customers' purchases.

He remembered Patterson's last minute instructions. "Don't spook him. Be patient. Wait for him to make a move, then signal us. We'll do the rest. Whatever you do, don't try cornering him by yourself."

Two of the sheriff's men were waiting in the parking lot, keeping an eye on Gary's truck and the rear entrance to the store. From their cruiser, they could pick up Troy's walkie-talkie signal. If the creep loaded his truck with stuff tonight, they'd be there to jump him the moment he pulled away. If it took a week or a month before his next snatch—they'd still be ready. Gary would have company round the clock.

As the last shoppers drifted toward exits at a few minutes before ten, Troy made another pass by Super-Charged. Jennifer's father was in there now, passing busily back and forth behind the display window. He was framed by CD's dangling on wires from the ceiling, four-foot-high stereo speakers, and a wide-screen TV. He spoke to Gary. Gary nodded and nodded again, looking serious.

"Gary old man, are you ever stringing your boss along," Troy muttered beneath his breath.

He wished he could listen in on their conversation. He hoped whatever happened, Jen's dad didn't get hurt. She'd never forgive him.

Troy checked his watch: 10:15. The regular guards would be making their rounds. Troy had told them he'd complete his usual task of securing the exits and locking the loading dock gates. He'd better get moving. If Gary pulled anything tonight, he didn't want to miss it. Although another theft wouldn't convince a jury he'd murdered two people, it would give the sheriff an excuse to arrest and interrogate him.

Chapter 16

JENNIFER DROVE SIXTY miles an hour along San Jacinto, her tires squealing as she veered around the corner into the mall access road. The moon was full, and her heart pounded like a sledgehammer in her chest when she spotted one of the sheriff's cruisers parked behind a row of trash dumpsters. Hoping the person inside the car hadn't seen her, she jammed her foot on the brake and swung the Miata around 180 degrees to head for the opposite side of the mall.

I have to get to Troy before Dad gets to him! she thought desperately.

"The young man who works in the electronics store," Joshua had said. Troy had assumed he meant Gary. But Joshua was an old man, in his sixties. To him, a man in his early forties would seem young. Frank Merrill was forty-two.

Her car skidded to a stop beside the security entrance. Jennifer bolted from behind the wheel and ran breathlessly up the steps to the door. She pulled on the handle. It was locked.

Fear rising in her like the hot desert wind, she pounded on the heavy metal door. It vibrated loudly beneath her fists, but no one answered. The guard on duty was either making his rounds or napping. Attacking the door again, she kept up her assault until her fists throbbed.

Jennifer tried to remember other entrances into the

sprawling complex and eliminated the two main ones through the department stores. These would definitely be locked by now. By breaking the glass or forcing a door she'd trigger alarms and might be stopped by other security guards before she could locate Troy. Every second counted now. She didn't have time for complicated explanations.

There was a back door for each store. These too would be bolted and alarmed. She could think of no other way in—except through a loading dock—and chances were these were also locked. Unless . . . unless Gary and her father were using the one directly behind SuperCharged at this very minute. From there she could not only get in but be in the best location to help Troy.

But first she had to get past the cruiser without being spotted.

Jennifer studied the exterior of the building. A silvery moon illuminated this side of the mall, which meant that the rear wall should be in deep shadow. She glanced down at her indigo jeans and navy blue sweatshirt. Good choice—dark colors wouldn't be easily spotted in the dark. She removed her white Reeboks with their glowing safety patches and her white socks.

Staying close to the cement wall, Jennifer ran, her heart crashing like thunder in her ears. The night was hot for October. Sweat beaded her upper lip and trickled down the crease of her spine.

As she rounded the corner, she could just make out the gleam of moonlight on metal from behind the dumpsters. But anyone standing on the loading dock would be unaware of the cruiser. Jennifer crouched low and kept moving.

At last she arrived at the cement ramp. Both her father's car and Gary's truck were parked alongside. No one was in sight, but the metal gate hadn't yet been secured for the night. *Good,* she thought, *that means Troy hasn't completed his rounds.* With any luck she was in time. She tried the ordinary door beside the much wider garage-style entrance.

"Yes-s-s," she breathed when the knob turned easily in her hand.

Opening the door a crack, Jennifer slipped soundlessly into the passage lit overhead by one bare bulb. The door clanked shut behind her with a wickedly hollow sound. Beneath her shirt, the sweat felt suddenly cold and clammy against her skin, and she began to tremble. She almost turned around and ran back out the way she'd come. This was the same place her father had nearly killed her.

The fact that he'd mistaken her for a stranger made no difference. *His* strength fighting against her own had overcome her. *His* hands had bruised her throat. Except for chance, she would have died six weeks ago.

And she might die tonight if she ran into her father before she found Troy. She no longer trusted him. He might weigh all of his options and decide that the life of his daughter wasn't as valuable to him as his own freedom.

It's not too late to turn around . . . run to the cruiser . . . tell them everything you know! a voice from inside her pleaded.

Without warning, the bulb above her head went out.

"Dad?" she called out hoarsely. "Dad, it's me, Jenny. I have to talk to you. Please."

She froze, not daring to move further than the few feet she'd already come. Feeling disoriented in the dark, she stretched out one hand to touch the wall on her left.

She tried to remember where everything was. On the right should be the open storage space for merchandise. Ten feet ahead would be the loading dock door that slid up on rails to a twelve-foot-high ceiling.

"Dad!" she cried, louder. "I have to talk to you!"

She imagined she heard voices, whispering not far away. But she couldn't make out the words.

Then the light flickered on.

Gary Pyzik stood in front of her with one hand on the light switch, the black pupils of his eyes grotesquely dilated.

"Go home, Jennifer," he ground out. "Your father doesn't want to talk to you."

"He *has* to!" she cried.

"He's busy. We have some things to take care of." His glance drifted to his right.

She could just make out a dim figure at the end of the passageway, its head behind the open door of a fuse box.

"I'll go to the sheriff!" she threatened loudly enough for her father to hear.

Gary squinted at her and ran his tongue over his lips, suddenly worried. "Did you hear that, sir?"

"She's bluffing. Keep her out of here!"

Intending to knock Gary out of her way, Jennifer rushed at him. He managed to stand his ground and grabbed her around the waist, at the same time pinning her arms to her sides.

"Let me go!" She swung her right knee sharply into his groin.

"Shit!" he yelled, releasing her.

Before he could catch his breath or straighten up, she drove her heel into his instep. Gary hopped on one foot, holding himself and moaning. But somehow he still managed to block the narrow passage.

"She won't leave!" he groaned. "What do you want me to *do?*"

"I don't care, you idiot!" Mr. Merrill shouted. "Just keep her out of my hair for five more minutes. I'll deal with her then."

Gary watched her warily, as if afraid she might attack him again but aware that he couldn't do anything to hurt her while his boss was nearby.

Jennifer crouched like a linebacker preparing to dash through a gap in the opposing team's defense. "If you let him get away with this, you'll go to jail, Gary," she taunted.

"Not me!" He glanced over his shoulder nervously. "Jen, I swear it was all his idea. Just a little extra cash under the table, that's what he said. He gave me the stuff to sell in Houston to some guy who fences stolen goods. We split the profit, and your father collected the insurance money. No one was supposed to get hurt."

"But people did," she reminded him.

"I didn't know about the old lady and Pete Foley until a month ago. By then it was too late."

"You were an accomplice," she accused him. "You kept your mouth shut when you knew what he'd done! And you tried to kill Troy!"

"I had no choice!" he hissed. "Your old man said he'd make it look like I'd done it all if I didn't help him." For the first time Gary looked as if he regretted his decision. "This way, we finish off clean. With Troy out of the picture, the sheriff won't have a case. Your dad and I have a deal." He smiled weakly. "He's giving me money . . . a lot of money to go to Mexico. Without any witnesses or proof, this mess will blow over. In a year or so, I can come back to Texas. Maybe open my own store in Houston or somewhere else. Hell, I won't even have to go to college to be rich!"

"You dummy!" she cried. "Troy is working for the sheriff and has been tailing you. If anything happens to him—every deputy in the county will figure you were behind it. My father is setting you up, Gary. You'll never be able to come home. You'll have to hide out for the rest of your life!"

Gary frowned, looking confused. "I . . . I don't believe you."

Jennifer shook her head in disbelief. "Someone as smart as you should be able to see what's going on." She took a step forward and lowered her voice to a threatening growl. "I'm going to talk to my father now. Move, or I'll claw your eyes out."

Gary must have believed her. Looking suddenly desperate, he stared first up then down the passage, as if hoping to spot a weapon. But there was nothing, only a half dozen empty soda bottles and a cardboard pizza box sitting on top of a pile of stereo receivers. With a gleam of inspiration in his eyes, Gary glanced at her bare feet.

Jennifer guessed what he was about to do the second before he made his move. "No!" she shrieked.

Seizing three bottles by their necks in each hand, he heaved them at the cement floor. Bright green splinters flew, and Jennifer jumped back. Between them lay a sparkling carpet of jagged glass.

"What the hell happened?" her father shouted from the end of the tunnel.

Gary grinned with satisfaction and sat down on a packing crate. "Everything's under control now, sir. I just made sure she won't bother you!"

Jennifer stared in horror at the hundreds of razor sharp shards in her path. She couldn't run around them or jump over them. Her feet would be torn to shreds if she tried to cross the floor.

Peering down the dimly lit passage, she saw her father stand away from the fuse box and brush his palms against his shirt, finished with his task. And suddenly she knew what he'd done.

Troy would circle the mall from the outside, checking to be sure all doors were locked, closing the metal gate across each loading dock. When he came to the one behind SuperCharged and touched it, thousands of volts would sizzle through his body. He couldn't possibly survive.

It took only a minute to decide what she had to do.

Glancing one last time at Gary, Jennifer focused on the far end of the tunnel . . . then she ran forward . . . straight over a six-foot stretch of broken glass.

Fiery claws of pain ripped through the soles of her

feet. Jennifer slowed down but didn't stop. Slivers must have embedded themselves in her flesh. Each step drove them deeper into the tender skin.

Tears streaming down her cheeks, she rushed at her father.

He caught her in his arms and held her tightly against his chest. "That was foolish, Jennifer," he scolded. "I wish you hadn't done that. If you weren't so upset and confused, I'm sure you wouldn't side with some boy over your own father."

"I won't let you kill him!" she wailed.

His voice remained eerily calm. "I'm afraid I can't let you talk me out of it. Things have gotten out of hand. Your mother, you, and I are leaving McCarter tonight. I've already closed out my local bank accounts and transferred the money to another state. You'll know which one when we get there. You'll like your new home and make new friends." He sounded as if she'd scraped her knee and he was comforting her, promising an ice cream cone if she'd stop crying.

"I won't go with you!" she cried, fighting his restraining arms.

"You will. We're a family. I've given you everything, Jennifer. Don't forget that. You owe me your loyalty."

He's absolutely insane, she thought, her stomach knotting. But something inside of her refused to let her give up. "The police will track you down."

"I doubt they'll bother. The only evidence they have are statements from two bums, who have since disappeared, made to a college kid moonlighting as a security guard. And he will soon have a terrible accident."

"The sheriff will find the wiring!" she shouted wildly. Anything to make him reconsider . . . anything to save Troy!

"Don't worry, the wiring will burn itself out within seconds after the young man touches the door. There will be no evidence of tampering." He called to Gary at the end of the tunnel, "Your money is in the envelope on my desk. You go on ahead."

"Yes, sir!" Gary gave him a lopsided grin as he leaned through the office door then left by way of the loading dock door.

"He hasn't figured it out, has he?" Jennifer whispered. "If he ever comes back to McCarter, he'll be blamed for everything."

Her father glanced down at her. "You're a smart girl."

"I hate you," she growled.

Troy's walkie-talkie buzzed on his hip. He pushed the call button and spoke into it. "Black, here."

"Pyzik just got into his truck and is driving across the parking lot. We're following. Consider yourself off-duty. Over."

"Right. Over."

Troy consulted his watch. Almost eleven and he hadn't finished securing the entrances around the mall. He'd been so tense all night, watching Gary, that he'd worked at a snail's pace. But now that the kid had left under the surveillance of the deputies, he felt as if he could relax while finishing his job.

Troy walked through the dark, humming a song he'd heard earlier on the radio, chasing shadows away with his flashlight. On the loading dock behind Betty's Bakery he checked to be sure the inside door was locked then grabbed the front of the steel accordion gate and ran with it, sliding the metal bar into its latch. He locked it with a key on his belt then rattled the gate for good measure.

Troy circled around the back side of the mall and was surprised to find Mr. Merrill's silver BMW still parked near the ramp close to SuperCharged. He hesitated, unsure if he should shut the gate with Jennifer's dad still inside the building.

Just then, a loud thumping sound came from the Merrill's car.

"What the—" he murmured. Curious, he stepped forward just as the car roared to life, its headlights shooting yellow streaks across the parking lot.

"All right to lock up, Mr. Merrill?" Troy called out.

But the car started to pull away. Apparently Jennifer's father hadn't heard him. Troy shrugged and continued up the cement ramp toward the security gate.

The moon cast a dense shadow along the side of the building. Troy propped the flashlight on the ground beside his feet so that he could see what he was doing. He pulled out his keys on the retractable cord attached to his belt and reached for the metal gate.

Inside the cramped trunk of the BMW where her father had stuffed her, Jennifer struggled helplessly against the tight loops of packaging tape. Her feet burned, still bleeding, she supposed, for they felt damp and horribly sticky. She'd screamed and beat her fists on the underside of the trunk hood until she was out of breath and her hands went numb, but she had no idea whether anyone had heard her.

Please let Troy hear! Please make him suspicious enough to investigate before he touches that gate!

She felt the car jiggle as her father climbed in and slammed the door. The engine started. Slowly, the car rolled away from the mall.

"Oh, Troy," Jennifer sobbed, swallowing salty tears. "I'm sorry . . . s-s-so sorry . . . I blew it . . ." If only she'd gone straight to the sheriff's men and told them about her father.

Strangely, it was at that moment that something Ben Derby had said to her on the tennis court replayed in her mind: "Don't let one missed shot take the match from you. Forget it. Make the next shot your best."

There had to be some way out of this nightmare!

She rolled onto her side, then to her knees and hands. Arching her back like a cat, Jennifer pressed up against the trunk hood.

Nothing.

All right, Mr. Smart Ben—now what? A backhand? She considered the possible weaknesses of the car construction. A BMW? Weak? The vehicle was a tank! The latch itself was probably the most vulnerable link, and that would certainly withstand her fiercest kicks, even if she'd had shoes on and her feet weren't bleeding all over the place.

By now she must have lost considerable blood. Maybe that was why she felt dizzy. Or maybe it was the lack of oxygen in the trunk, or exhaust fumes seeping into the compartment . . .

Concentrate! You've got to get out to warn Troy!

What kind of tools were stored in the trunk that might multiply her strength? She felt around in the carpeted space. A package of flares . . . jumper cable . . . gallon of windshield washer fluid . . . None of them would do her any good. A couple maps . . . tire jack . . . a—

The tire jack! Her fingers traced the metal outline. The long handle was shaped almost like a crowbar. If she could wedge it into the crack, she might be able to force the latch.

She heard Troy call out to her father just as the car started to move faster! But he'd never be able to hear her over the sound of the engine. In a few seconds, he'd touch the gate and . . .

She wouldn't let herself think about that.

Working quickly, Jennifer jammed the jack into the crevice and leaned on it with her full weight.

The trunk creaked, groaned, at last popped open.

Jennifer scrambled to her knees and rolled out of the trunk, tucking her shoulder to break her fall from the moving vehicle. She landed with an awful jolt, her forehead striking the pavement, stunning her. A sharp pain sliced through her chest.

"Troy!" she cried weakly. "Don't touch the gate!"

She pushed herself up onto her knees and stood. White-hot knives of pain slashed through the soles of her feet as the embedded slivers pressed deeper into her flesh. She collapsed on the ground in agony. Her head spinning, tears clouding her vision, she crawled on hands and knees toward the dock.

Unfortunately, Troy didn't seem to see her.

The BMW stopped, appeared to hesitate for a moment, then turned around and roared back in her direction. Tears streaked down Jennifer's face as she watched the headlights swell, heading straight for her.

But the car swerved at the last moment, driving past her, pulling up beside the loading dock. She watched helplessly, unable to stand again on her injured feet with the hope of making herself visible to Troy.

Her father got out of his car, walked around to the back, and reached into the open trunk.

Although her ribs hurt terribly, Jennifer took a deep breath and forced out a ragged scream, "Troy, run! Get away from him! He did it! He did it all!"

Troy must have heard at least a few words of her warning. He stared at Frank Merrill, coming up the ramp toward him with the jack in his hand. Pulling his gun slowly from the shoulder holster, Troy backed away until he was almost touching the gate.

As Jennifer sank down on the cold pavement, her vision blurred. She saw her father charge at Troy, brandishing the jack. Troy stepped aside, aiming his gun at Frank Merrill's chest . . . but he never fired. The man's momentum carried him straight into the metal mesh. The jack touched the gate, a vivid flash brightened the night, and a loud crackling sound filled the air.

Frank Merrill let out a shout of surprise and stiffened for ten seconds before dropping limply to the ground.

Chapter 17

JENNIFER WALKED ALONG the highway two miles west of McCarter into the desert. She found a familiar rocky ledge, bordered by wild yucca trees and prickly pears, and sat down to watch the sun set beyond the twin knolls. The desert was beautiful at dusk. As the sun melted on the horizon, the heat of the day dissolved into cool, soothing shadows. And the red glow in the west faded to purple and gold.

A few silvery specks peeked out before the sky was completely dark. Then suddenly night was all around her, thick and black with thousands of brilliant stars sprinkled over her head.

This was the first time Jennifer had left her house since the night her father died. Reporters had staked out the Merrill home from the moment news of the mall murders broke. They'd pushed microphones at her and turned cameras on her face as they asked, "Did your father really try to kill you?" and "What does it *feel* like to be the daughter of a murderer?"

She and her mother had stopped answering the door and let the machine screen all telephone calls. Neither of them had slept for days.

Jennifer rubbed the bandages that taped the three ribs that had cracked when she rolled out of the car trunk. She still wore soft socks and moccasins to cushion her healing feet, but they no longer hurt when she walked. She thought about Gary Pyzik, who'd broken the bottles that had shredded her skin. The authorities had arrested him for theft, attempted murder, and a long list of other criminal charges. If the prosecuting attorney couldn't make one stick, he or she would get a conviction on another.

Jennifer blocked out thoughts of Gary and her father. What she needed now was time to herself, time to sort things out. Her whole life had gone down the toilet. There was no one who could possibly understand . . . no one she dared share her feelings with. She felt so ashamed for her family.

Jennifer sat in the deepening darkness of the desert, and time passed.

Something touched Jennifer's shoulder as she lay curled up on her side. Hard ground, not her own soft mattress pressed into her hip. She felt stiff and cold. Opening her eyes, she sat up, surprised to find the sun shining.

"Jen?" It was Patty. Her smooth brown face was contorted with worry.

"How'd you find me?" she asked.

"We used to come here, remember? To tell secrets."

"Well, I don't have any more secrets . . . the whole world knows," Jennifer added with a sigh. "Go away. Leave me alone."

"No," Patty said stubbornly. "No matter what else has happened, we can still be friends. That will never change."

"Are you sure you want to be friends with the daughter of a murderer?"

Patty sat down beside her on the ledge. "Why not? *You* didn't do anything wrong. Nobody blames you for what your father did."

Jennifer hung her head, feeling miserable. "I lived with him all of my life. I should have known."

"I don't see how." Patty hesitated. "I thought you

might like to know. Louise and Ben got back together. They make a great couple. Ben's a different person—he hasn't looked at another girl all week."

Jennifer gave her a half smile. "That's great. I hope they're happy." She hesitated. "You didn't come all the way out here to tell me about Ben though."

"No," Patty admitted. "Jen, there's someone who wants to see you."

"Who?"

"Troy."

Jennifer groaned. "I can't . . . oh, jeez . . . Not after all the terrible things I thought about him. And when he asked me not to tell anyone who he was and why he was in McCarter . . . what did I do? I ran off and blabbed everything to my father, the last person in the world who should have known."

"But it wasn't intentional," Patty objected.

"Intentional or not, I nearly got Troy killed. I can't face him. Tell him I won't see him."

"You'll have to tell him yourself," Patty said, standing up. "He's right over there."

Jennifer twisted around, her heart racing. Troy's pickup truck was parked off the side of the road. He and Mike leaned against the bumper, watching them.

"No," Jennifer breathed.

"You can do it. Come on!" Grabbing her hand, Patty pulled her toward the truck.

Troy stepped forward to meet her. "How are you doing?" he asked, his solemn gray eyes searching her face. In jeans and a plaid western shirt he looked more like an ordinary high school boy than an FBI agent-in-training.

"All right . . . better," she said.

Mike put an arm around Patty and remarked, "Jennifer, you look awful."

"That's not nice!" Patty scolded, elbowing him in the ribs.

"Well, she does!" he objected. "She looks like she hasn't slept in a month and probably feels like the loser of a prize fight. Why not come right out and say it!"

Mike's dark eyes met Jennifer's, and she could read in them his honest sympathy. Somehow, she suddenly felt a little less guilty for everything that had happened.

"You're right," she murmured. "That's exactly how I feel . . . like I've been chewed up and spit out. Thanks, Mike."

"No sweat." He laughed. "Guess I've felt like that plenty of times myself."

Jennifer smiled weakly. "I wish I knew what to say to you all." She turned to Troy. "I'm sorry . . . I should have trusted you. And I should never have told my father your secret . . . I-I still feel terrible about that."

"In your place, I would have done the same thing," Troy assured her. "You thought you were protecting him. You had no idea what kind of man he was."

She nodded, not totally forgiving herself but glad that Troy could.

Then she looked at Mike. "I don't know what to say . . ." She had to swallow twice before she was able to force out her next words. "My father killed Pete."

"I know," Mike said.

Tears filled her eyes and rolled down her cheeks. "There's nothing I can do to bring him back. You even got cheated out of your revenge."

Slowly, Mike nodded. "I've been thinking a lot about that lately. You know, as time passes, hurting somebody else to pay back for Pete . . . well, that seems to make less and less sense. You're right, nothing's going to bring back my brother. That leaves me as the only son in my family." He shook his head solemnly. "Sort of puts a lot of pressure on me to do good . . . you know, make my mom and dad proud and be there for them if they need me."

"That's a nice way of thinking of it," Jennifer said, softly sniffling.

"Yeah." He looked at Troy. "I thought I might do something Pete would have done if he'd been around . . . you know, to like keep his memory alive? He was always good with little kids. Maybe I'll help out with peewee football, show 'em how to really kick the old ball."

Patty squeezed him and smiled. "I think Pete would have liked that," she murmured.

Jennifer studied her friend's pretty face. She'd always admired Patty for her kindness and intelligence, but now Jennifer remembered that she'd learned something about her that she didn't like.

"Are you two going to Homecoming?" she asked impulsively, thinking of the red dress.

Patty shot her a panic-stricken look.

"Homecoming?" Mike asked. "Why would you think—" He glanced at Patty. "Oh, she means that you want to go?"

Patty shrugged. "Well . . . I might, if the right person asked me."

"I'd have to rent a tux," Mike mused out loud. "But I've been putting money aside from my paychecks for a while. I can afford it. You got something to wear?"

Patty glowed. "Do I ever! I even applied for my first charge card so I could buy a gown. I may be making payments for six months, but it'll be worth it!"

"What?" shrieked Jennifer. "You didn't *steal* the red dress?"

Patty rolled her eyes. "Are you crazy? I wouldn't do anything like that! Did you really think I stole it?"

"I guess I did," Jennifer admitted sheepishly.

"I was so scared my parents would find out about the charge card, I didn't even dare tell you. I figured one of us would let something slip. They'd say I was being irresponsible, spending money I didn't have. But I promised myself that I won't spend another penny until that dress is paid off."

"Good for you," Jennifer said.

Troy coughed lightly, as if to get her attention. Jennifer faced him.

"Will you take a short walk with me over to the knolls?" he asked.

"I . . . I don't know," Jennifer said cautiously. She felt her heart begin to beat a little faster as he gazed down at her. She didn't want to take the chance of being hurt again if all he intended to do was repeat his good-bye speech.

"Mike and I will wait at the truck," Patty said quickly, her eyes twinkling. "Go ahead. We can all drive back into town together when you're done chatting."

Troy took Jennifer's hand, and they walked in silence across the parched ground toward the gentle mounds covered with scrub grass and prickly pears. Some people thought the desert was ugly. Jennifer thought it was dramatic and full of surprises, like life.

"I drove by your house yesterday," Troy began. "I saw the For Sale sign out front. Guess I wanted to know if you'll be staying around McCarter or moving away to be with relatives."

"As soon as the house sells, my mom and I will probably rent an inexpensive apartment somewhere in town, at least for awhile."

"And after that?" Troy asked.

"I don't know. I can't imagine living anywhere but McCarter . . . except maybe to go away to college," Jennifer explained, wondering why Troy was so curious about her future. "Even if my mother wanted to leave, I'd try to stay and graduate with my friends."

Troy nodded thoughtfully. He didn't speak for several minutes, then continued in a taut voice. "When I was helping out the sheriff, I told you I wasn't looking for a girlfriend."

"I remember," she said.

"Well, I just wanted to let you know that my internship with the sheriff's office is over. And I'm still not looking for a girlfriend . . . but here you are and—" He cleared his throat nervously and brushed a chunk of blond hair off of his forehead, "What I'm trying to say is that I want to see you again, Jennifer . . . if you'd like to see me."

Suddenly, her whole body felt wonderfully warm, and she smiled at Troy. "I'd like that. But what about your school? You're going back to college, aren't you?"

"Oh, sure. I'll have classes during the week, just like you. But there are always weekends, and we can talk on the phone between Sunday and Friday."

Jennifer reached up around Troy's neck and pressed her cheek to his heart to hear it beat a comforting rhythm.

"You're alive," she whispered gratefully.

"Yup." He gave her a warm hug.

"I don't know how everything worked out this way, but it doesn't matter," she murmured. "If life is going to be a little tougher from now on, at least I have friends to help me through."

Troy touched his lips to the top of her head. "Count on it."